LUXURY BOYZ

Michael Robinson

Luxury Boyz Publishing
Ontario, California

Luxury Boyz: Michael Robinson
Copyright © 2022 by Michael Robinson.

ISBN - Paperback: 978-1-7355175-1-3
          E-Book: 978-17355175-0-6

Published by Luxury Boyz Publishing
              1056 E. Philadelphia St. #L104
              Ontario CA 91761
              Luxuryenterprises77@gmail.com

Cover Design: For Union Sign Company
Editing and Formatting: Visual Bridge Designs

All rights reserved
First printing 2022
Library of Congress Control Number: 2021904923
Printed and bound in the United States of America.

Special Dedication

To my gifts from God; my wife to be Angel and my new chapter in my life Mi'Kah ... Daddy can't wait to kiss you .

To the brothers I have from different mother's. Salutes troops you know who you are.

Now last but not least I dedicate this book to all the Luxury Boyz worldwide. Keep your eyes on the prize. Know where you are going

Thank you to God, who will never leave me.

Amen 777 Born

Acknowledgments

Observance to my Heavenly Father and the Son, Jesus Christ, my savior. Thank you for always protecting me, for giving me the opportunity to serve you, and giving me the mind to express my frustrations through creative writing and imagination...

To my first-born My'Kara. Please forgive me for making mistakes that got me ten years in federal prison. Remember to talk to the Most High above about everything good and bad. Your Dads' love is unconditional and forevermore.

To my first-born son, Michael Motto, Remember what your pops told you. Keep the Most High in all that you do. Don't surrender to anything but God. Keep your head up, eyes on your prize and go get it. Ain't no one giving you anything. Life is full of lessons. Take notes and take nothing for granted.

I would like to say give respect to the people who made me: my parents Big Mike (the gorilla) and Patricia "Sweet Necey". First Dad: I love and miss you. Thanks for the heart you gave me, the knowledge you inbreed in me. I know you are in heaven and we will meet again. Momma you are truly a gift from God. Your strength and unconditional love has made me a solider for real. Thank you for all the talks that I didn't want to hear. Love you forever.

Thanks to all who have been here through the whole struggle. Special dedication to my number one fan; my Auntie Lydia. Miss you so much Auntie. I think of you daily. Thanks for always being there for me. You are truly missed.

Thanks to Saquana, the first person to call me Luxury Boy. Even though we aren't together, thank you for being there for me like no one had before.

Lil Kim, Tiffany, Monique, Von, Tessa, Rendie, and Trice, thanks for being the sisters I never had. Yawl are my sisters for life.

Rest in peace to all my love ones—Big Mike, Big Flipp, Big Motto, Manky One, Shadow Locc, Jay Locc, both of my grandparents and G-Mom Johnnie Mae. Miss you Granny.

The Luxury Boyz team and staff salutes: my agents, editors, formatter and cover designer. Thanks for your professional work and support.

Chapter 1

It took some time getting use to the move to the city. On my third day there, I had a fight with Pelle, because Raven, the girl who lived next door, liked me and Pelle used to be her boyfriend. He threw a dirt rock at me and hit me on the back of my head. The M.C. Hammer baggy pants I wore must've made him think that I was a punk. Little did he know, I had a very short and stubborn temper. I picked up a solid rock and threw it with an underhand throw that I learned when I played baseball. It hit his nose and blood streamed down his face as he dashed at me. We fought until my mom came out and broke it up. Then we both just mad dogged each other with hard, mad stares! ***That started a friendship that lasted a lifetime!*** Pelle was no punk and neither was I.

The next morning Pelle knocked on my door.

My mom answered with, "Boy, you coming roun' here for trouble?"

Pelle was not rude, instead he apologized to my mom and then asked if I could go out. We sat on the porch and talked.

"Hey, Raven says your name is 'Mista'. Is it?"

"Yeah," I replied.

"Why they call you that?"

"My real name is 'Mutasur'. My folks said that ever since I was little I acted mature, so my momma nicknamed me 'Mista'. Why they call you 'Pelle'?"

"Cause my real name is 'Shapelle', 'Pelle' is short for my real name." We got up and walked to the front gate.

"Where y'all move from?"

"We moved from the valley."

"Oh—where all the White peoples stay?"

"Yeah! But it's Blacks out there too."

"Yeah, the ones with money. What y'all move to the hood for?"

"My momma left her boyfriend and my grand momma is sick. That's why we moved in with her."

"Why you wearing those M.C. Hammer pants?"

"Cause I like them. Why? You got a problem with em?"

"No, but ... well, Mista, the homies around here gonna talk about you wearing those. 'Specially if you go to school like that, man. You need some Jordans, some Nikes and some Reeboks. Where yo momma work?"

"She works for the state, at the City Hall. Where you go get your birth records at."

"Oh, I've been there before with my moms. Damn! Your moms work there? She can buy you lots of Jordans and shit!"

"I got some Nike's and Jordans. I just like sandals and these pants."

"Well, go put on some Jays and some sweatpants so we can get to Rocks house in the hood."

"Who is Rock? And what hood?"

"Luxury Boyz, and you one now. Rock's real name is 'Robert'. They call him Rock cause his two brothers stay socking him and he don't cry or tell his mom. He just hit back, and he hits hard—like a rock. Go change your shoes and put some sweats on, so we can go on Luxury Street to his house."

When we got there both of Rock's brothers, Q-Ball and Lil Q, were on the porch with some others smoking weed and drinking beer. Lil Q said, "Rock's in the club house."

When we walked in, Rock was standing up with his pants and boxers lowered to his ankles, getting his dick sucked by a grown lady, who was on her knees. She didn't even look up at us. She just kept on bobbin' her head up and down.

Rock said, "What up, Pelle-Pelle, you want next? Who is that?"

"My cousin Mista. He just moved in two houses down from me. Hell yeah—I want next! What about you Cuz?"

"Who me? Yeah! Oh, yea-yeah ... me too!"

When Rock was done, Pelle stood in front of her. Rock gave him a crack rock to give to her. Pelle handed it to her, then said, "Give me a condom, Cuz!"

"You don't need no condom, Pelle." Q-Ball said. "You can't catch shit like that. Only from fucking!"

I was next. I stood there and pulled down my pants. I didn't want to seem scared, but I was. She looked at my dick and started sucking.

She stopped and said, "Damn boy, you got a big dick. How old is you?"

"I'm twelve."

Every day after school we went to the clubhouse, and got some head from the neighborhood "head doctor". That's what we called her.

$

Three Years Passed

We all had mini bikes. Mines—my moms bought, but Pelle's and Rock's were stolen. We wanted this Mini Blazer that cost $1600, so we sold our bikes for $600. We came up with a plan to sell weed out of the clubhouse to get the rest of the money. Q-Ball and Lil Q-Ball went to jail before we could buy our supply from them. So we went to where Q-Balla use to cop his shit from, at Oscar's house. Oscar lived a few blocks away from the hood. Cholo was Oscar's nephew. We went to school with Cholo, so Oscar took good care of us—really good; he gave us half dope and half weed for $600.

We didn't know how much to give, so we gave our customers what we thought fit. Little did we know we were giving them more than the regular amount, so that brought people way from the east and south sides to us. We were taking other people customers. We started making so much money, it was like—wow! We bought the Mini Blazer. It was all of ours. We got sounds for it ... some clothes and shoes for ourselves, and got a re-up from Cholo. Raven became my girl. Pelle had her best friend Kimy. Rock, ooh—you know! He was the playboy of the bunch.

Rock paged me with our emergency code 777, which is three L's upside-down. I wasted no time calling him back.

"They robbed me! They robbed me! Get over here!" He yelled.

"I'm going to get Pelle," I said.

When we got there, Rock was drinking some old rotgut whiskey—shit the old heads and bums drank.

"Damn, man! What you drinking that shit for?" I said.

"Cause, I don't want to be in my right mind when I kill them fools."

"What fools? Who robbed you?"

"It was them older niggas Lamont and Capone—Man—and the Greenland clique!"

Rock passed me the bottle then walked out of the clubhouse to a hole where his brother's guns were buried. He dug up a large bag of guns and took them inside the club house. I passed the drink to Pelle. Rock pulled out the guns and tossed me one, then Pelle, and put one on his waist.

"We can't ever get caught slipping without our heat, ever. We ain't got no works or money. They took everything. If we go get they ass back, take our shit back, and their shit, then we will be back up. So, what? Y'all wanna go do this shit or what?" Rock said.

"Them fools got us broke. Nigga, hell yeah! This the "L". Let's get them niggas!"

"Yeah, let's get they ass back!"

"We gonna go hit they spot and then open up two shops on Luxury Street!"

We jumped in the Blazer and rolled straight to the Greenland hood.

"Look man, this how we gonna do this shit. We gonna act like we wanna know if they heard something. Act like we don't know it was them niggas, man. Cause they think since they had on masks, I don't know it was them. Yeah, but I seen the watch that nigga Lamont always wears," Rock said.

We parked across the street from their spot and waited. When we got out of the Blazer, it was two in the morning. The street was clear. There was nobody outside but the Greenland niggas. When we walked up to Peanut, he said, "Shit man, I don't know who got y'all. I bet you niggas won't be flossing no more."

There were two dudes out front. Pelle said that he had them covered. When we got to the door, Lamont's punk ass opened it. I just pulled and fired. He didn't expect to see me at his front door. So he never had a chance to react. We blasted our way in, shooting everything and everybody inside. Then we searched for our shit. Poo Bear killed dead in the kitchen while he was counting money that they must have just gotten. We found all our shit, bagged everything and got ghost. Pelle was waiting in the Blazer with the motor running. We jumped in and speed off.

We went to the clubhouse to see what we got. We came up good. We got our three pounds of weed and our four ounces of powder back. But them niggas was sitting on some weight! We got from them eighty pounds of weed, and ten keys of powder, plus cash—$140,000. Nobody cared that Lamont and his crew got their hat brung to them, because they were the ones robbing and breaking in everybody's houses.

We all had medallion necklaces made that read Luxury Boy and got Rolex watches with our initials engraved on them.

$

Three Years Later

We had four houses on Luxury Street rolling like clock-work. Raven and I had a little girl. We lived in Claremont, an upscale area, in a four bedroom house. Rock and Q-Ball's mom lived in two of the houses on Luxury Street that were not a spot. The other two were safe houses. Pelle bought his mom a house and himself a condominium in a gated community. Q-Ball and Lil Q got out of jail. Lil Q stayed with Rock, and Q-Ball had his mom's house remolded and added what he called the 'Players Wing' on to it for himself. For some reason he wouldn't leave his mom's house.

We all got whips. I drove a Jaguar, Pelle an Escalade EXT, Q-Baller drove a Beamer 650, Lil Q got himself a 320 Benz, and Money drove a Lexus. Paper was being made and things were all good. But like they say, 'Good things don't last too long'.

All the money boys would hang out at the Square on Fridays—a parking lot of: a liquor store, nail shop, burger spot and a fish place. All the ballers would bring their whips to floss: low riders, luxury cars, big trucks, bikes and race cars. The air smelled like smoking tires and kush weed all night.

We rode to the square in our R.V. that we got from a clucker that owed us some paper. He gave it to us to hold until he was able to pay up, but we had no intentions on giving it back. So we had it costumed up from the inside out—the outside read Luxury. We didn't floss our cars anymore. We would pull up to the square in our house on wheels and hang out there until we drove to Vegas; which we did every weekend. Kelly, the home girl, was our personal driver. She didn't drink; she just smoked.

I passed the lovely to Pelle, that's kush weed dipped in sherm (PCP), and was sipping my Remy, when a forest green Corvette pulled up across the street from us. D-Money jumped out.

"That's Lamont's brother. That nigga we killed. He acting like he don't see us," I said.

D-Money had money. He was the reason Lamont and all of the Greenland niggas had anything to begin with. He went to the Feds for five years. That's the reason why the clique became jack-boys. D-Money walked around his car to the passenger side and leaned on the door. Then Stacey walked up to him. Pelle had been fucking Stacey when D-Money was locked down. I tapped Pelle.

"Look Nigga, that's D-Money and that bitch you been fucking, ain't it?"

"Yeah, that's that trick."

"You know that's his girl? They was together before he went to jail. Well Nigga, I hope that bitch don't know where you stay? And don't fuck with that trick no more! That nigga know we smoked his brother and his homies!"

"Man, Mista, I already told you that hoe. Don't speak on me with that, clown!"

"Yeah, ok, Nigga. Believe me. He wants revenge. Remember Q-Ball said he tried to stab him in the pen?"

Stacy got in the car on the passenger side and D-Money walked back around the car. This time he stared at us as if he wanted it right then. He jumped in his car and burned rubber speeding off. I was high as hell and tipsy.

"Let's roll," I said.

We hit the highway to Las Vegas for the weekend. Kelly was under the wheel. We stayed at the New York-New York Hotel and Casino so much, that our presence was wanted and well welcomed. Plus, Pelle, Q-Ball, and I gambled 24/7, so they would give us a presidential suite every weekend just for going down. As soon as we got there, we all showered, changed, and hit the crap tables. At 10 P.M. we went back to the room to smoke some lovely and chill. Kelly ordered room service for us—our usual; lobster, steak, prawns, shrimp, salad, Philly cheesesteak, baked potatoes, three bottles of Remy, and three bottles of Moet. As she made that order, I made the order for the main course of the night— four Asian bitches—to set it off early for Kelly's C-day. Kelly likes women too.

The next morning, I had a meeting with Mr. Salers, my realtor, to close the deal on a vacation house I was buying in Vegas. I woke Kelly up and told her to get dressed. Before we left, I woke Pelle up and told him to send them hoes on their way, and that Kelly and I would be back. Out front waiting for us was a jet-black Lambo that the hotel got for me. I got in and speed off. The gate opened automatically when we got to the gated mansion. The realtor had it motion censored for my arrival.

The house was beautiful. It cost way more than I expected, but I could not refuse it. There was a waterfall in the front yard and the front door was taller than most people's houses. The inside was like—wow! The floors were black, white and gray marble. There was a state-of-the-art chef style kitchen that took our breaths away, and seven bedrooms, each with their own bathrooms. The master bedroom was like a studio apartment by itself. It had in it a spa bath with soft shooters. There was a one-bedroom guest house and a pool house. The pool house was two and a half stories tall with an elevator. The bathrooms in it were made of waterfall marble. There was no need to look at any more houses. I knew this was the one. I had to have it. Mr. Salers handed me the keys and said his good-byes.

I took Kelly by the hand, looked in her eyes and told her, "Don't tell nobody about this spot, not even Pelle, Q, Rock or any of the other L-Boyz, okay?"

She was shocked that I turned her on to my private spot.

"Mista, what does this mean? Why don't you want the crew to know 'bout this place? Mista—why you bring me here?"

She looked seriously worried and very sexy as she stared in my eyes.

"Cause, evidently I know I can trust you. Right?"

"Yeah, Mista, you know that."

"Plus, I know you like me more than just for a homie."

I walked closer to her and stopped in front of her.

"Yeah, I know, but I'm Ravens friend!"

Before she could say another word, my tongue was in her mouth. I picked her up as she wrapped her arms around me. I sat her on the stainless-steel counter top and I spread her legs apart. I pulled up the lil' black dress and to my surprise she didn't have on any panties. I dived in tongue first. I kissed her thighs, and sucked on her clit till she shook and shook. I pulled her down to let her taste her juices on my lips. Then I turned her around and fucked the dog shit out of Kelly. Her pussy felt like virgin pussy. I wanted to burst as soon as I entered her. But, I held it back, and pumped harder and harder. The more she said my name, the more I tried to push my log through to the other side of her. Then I busted all in that pussy. We both caught our breath and laughed. On the way back to the hotel, I told her that her pussy was mine and only mine, and that place was for us. That she could have a bitch as long as she was willing to take on my dick too!

Back in the room we showered, got dressed, and called room service for food. Then we went out to gamble. I played the horses. I sat there and smoked imported cigars and sipped on Remy for twelve hours straight. Then we went back to the room for another smoke session. We smoked a lovely blunt and four chronic blunts, and then we went back to gambling. At 1 A.M. we went back to the room showered and changed. Then we walked across the bridge to the club inside the MGM hotel and partied till seven in the morning. After that, we went back to our room to have another smoke session and then everybody crashed out.

Kelly went to her room and I followed right behind her. She was looking sooo good. Earlier when we were leaving to go to the club, I wanted to say, *"Let's go back to the room while everybody is gone."* Kelly was bad: high yellow and her shape is like a Coca-Cola bottle—ass like a basketball! I found myself digging into Kelly's sweet juices for four hours. We fucked, made love, then fell into a deep coma sleep.

When Pelle woke up and didn't see me in my room, he went to see if Kelly was still in hers. He saw that I was in her bed and said, "Damn, it must be nice."

All we could say was, "Get out!"

After we ate and packed, we hit the highway and smashed back to the city. We went to the Park and Store storage where we parked the R.V. and had left the cars. As we all got ready to leave, I walked Kelly to her Benz truck and told her to call the number that I gave her. Mr. Salers would give her the address to the house, so she could get it fully furnished. Kelly was a down ass bitch. No punk to the trigger neither. She kept her slang on all the time. But we only let her make runs and count cash.

"All right Mista, see you at the party."

"Alright I'll be there with all the L Boys."

I smashed to the house, went straight to my daughter Magazine's room and kissed her on the forehead. I then went into the gym were I knew I would find Raven looking just as sexy as ever. She had on those tight stretch exercise pants that I liked to see her in. She jumped off the bike and ran towards me. My dick instantly got rock hard. She hugged me and said, "You missed mommy, huh?" Then she rubbed her hand across my stiff dick

"Yeah, all weekend," I said, as I undressed her.

I couldn't resist her caramel sweaty glistening skin. I picked her up and sat her on top of my log—the way she liked it. I stroked her like I was driving iron. She started oohing and awing, and told me that it was in her stomach. I laid her down on the weight bench and long stroked her till I was soaking wet—just like exercising on the bike or running on the treadmill.

Chapter 2

I walked into our bedroom, turned on the spa bath and rolled me a blunt. I then got in and smoked the blunt while I watched the world news. Raven came in after she showered. She bathed me from head to toe, then she got in the spa with me. She sure knows how to treat a nigga like a king. That's why I will always love her. When I stepped in the bedroom and she dried me off from head to toe, and rubbed me down with olive oil. That's when I noticed the new Jordans, and a white and purple Lakers warm-up jump suit.

"Who that for?" I asked.

"My man." she said, as she dropped down to her knees, took my log in her mouth and sucked me 'til all my juices shot down her throat. She let it run down her neck and rubbed it in her skin, then she jumped on my dick. Raven rode me like she was riding a horse. Afterwards, I got dressed fresher than fresh air, splashed on some of my favorite Polo cologne, then walked into the movie room where Raven was.

"Hey gorgeous you need anything?" I asked.

"All I need is you, Daddy."

"I love you too Babe. I will be back in five hours, okay? Gotta take care of some thangz".

I jumped in my 1964 Cutlass ragtop, the color was the same as the Lakers and it sat on twenty-two inch rims. I headed to the car wash, then I smashed to the city. Once on the freeway, I called B-Locc to make sure he would be ready. I honked seven times in front of his house to signal that I was there. He stepped out in an all brown linen suit and some brown Romeos.

He walked up, handed me his blunt and said, "Hey Mista, I thought you was rolling the Jaguar. I got two burners on me. We might get pulled over in this."

"Oh, mother fucker, that's why I got four stash spots that fits four guns in each one. Get in my nigga, let's roll out and get Jay Locc. I'm only staying four hours. Y'all can roll back with Q, Rock, Pelle and Young Money."

"Yeah, man, this party gonna be off the hook. All Kelly's celebrity friends gonna be there. Man, she having strippers, women and men for the hoes."

"Wow, it's going down tonight, nigga ..."

"Oh yeah, it's going down. Kelly rented a glass house mansion up in the Hollywood Hills."

We walked through the house towards the back. People were skinny dipping in the inside pool, giving lap dances, swinging from poles, eating pussy, sucking dicks. It was wild and it was not even 10 P.M. yet. Yeah! Kelly knew how to throw a party. We kept moving through to the next room that was in a club style set up. I saw my crew sitting at a lounge type table. We walked up and greeted them.

"What's luxury?" I said. "That's how we gonna always greet each other from now on."

"The L-Boyz' greeting." said Pelle.

I asked bout the Q brothers. Pelle said they was in a room fucking some hoes. As I walked around, I saw Kelly signaling me to come upstairs. I walked behind Kelly upstairs to the master bedroom that is the size of a studio apartment. I turned her around to face me.

"Happy C-day Kelly."

"Thanks Mista, I can't forget the way you fucked me in Vegas—out of my head." She was rubbing on my dick as she spoke.

"When I'm getting some more?"

"When you ready?" I replied.

"Huh, right now."

"Yeah, but later tonight. It's too many people running around right now. But this weekend for sho."

"I got to get use to this big dick you got Mista—mum, yeah," she said. We kissed and walked back downstairs.

I went and sat back with my L-Boyz crew, and poured myself a glass of Moet mixed with Remy. Pelle passed me a box of spiffs. I took one, lit it and took a nice puff of the purple kush. Then I sat back as this Asian broad came over and gave me a table dance.

She said, "Compliments of the birthday girl."

I relaxed in that feeling for a moment. We sat back and laughed and joked 'bout J-Locc on the floor dancing, when I saw Stacy tap Pelle.

"Look man, there goes that bitch, Stacy."

"Yeah, I saw that bitch earlier. She said she had been calling me since this weekend while we were in Vegas," said Pella.

"Nigga, I told you to leave that rat bitch alone. Nigga that pussy that good? Cause that bitch is trouble."

"Mista ... Cuz ... I got this. Don't trip. I'm gonna let that bitch suck my dick tonight, then go home with someone else," he replied.

"Yeah, Ok Nigga, whatever you say. Look Cuz, I gotta get back to wifey. I'm out. Rock, B-Locc make sure y'all keep an eye on Pelle. Pelle—he might be slipping and fucking with that trick bitch, Stacy over there." I pointed in their direction. "I'm out ... Seven."

I had Raven's sexy body on my mind. She's caramel, the perfect size and has the prettiest tits I've ever seen—pink nipples that make my dick rock hard every time I see them. I walked through the garage straight to my daughter Magazine's room and kissed her on the forehead. That's something I do every time I go home. Then I made my way to our bedroom. Raven sure knows how to turn me on. She was sitting in the bed reading her real estate book wearing a crouch less pink lingerie camisole with lace and hearts everywhere on it. Her fat pussy poked out—made my log swell.

"How's the real estate business going babe? You got mortgage to pay tonight?"

"Mista," she said and pulled me in the bed.

We wasted no time stripping me down to nothing. She asked if I was hungry.

"Yes and I'm about to eat." I said.

I pulled her to the end of the bed, pulled her panties off and ate what I had an appetite for. Raven hunched her back and grinded her pussy. I put the log in and twisted, turned, and grinded forever. That Remy had me where I couldn't even nut. So I flipped her over, gave it to her while she laid on her stomach. As I beat her from behind, my nuts was clapping on that pussy. That sound turned Raven on and made her cum, over and over again. Then I slid it in her ass to finish it off. I busted all up in that ass. Then I fell on her back. I felt stress free.

Raven got up to warm up dinner. She had made my favorite—shrimp spaghetti, salad, and crab legs. I ate and then fell into a coma sleep. My phone woke Raven. She never answered my phone, so she woke me. It was Rock. He said that Pelle got shot up and Jay Loc was dead. They were at the hospital.

"Damn! FUCK!"

"What's wrong baby?" Raven asked as I hung up the phone.

"Pelle got shot and Jay Loc is dead. I gotta go to the hospital," I said as I jumped to my feet.

"Do you want me to go with you?"

"No," I replied. "I don't want my family out. I don't know if those niggas might try something on me."

I got dressed with Raven's cum still dry on my dick. I put on all black and grabbed my Tech 9, my 32 Automatic and my Baby 45. I didn't know what was up, but I got ready for war. I jumped in my Jag and smashed to Lincoln Memorial. The desk receptionist told me, "Third floor." When I got off the elevator, I saw all the L Boys sitting with Mrs. Walters, Pelle's mom. His sister, Pam, who is a federal agent, and his ex-girlfriend Kimy was there too. She left him cause she didn't want to go through just what she was going through right now.

Mrs. Walter stood up to hug me with tears running down her face. She tried to talk, but couldn't. She just broke down. All I could say was, "It's gonna be okay. We gonna take care of you." Then I helped her sit down. I went to hug Pam.

"He was hit once in the leg, the hip once, and once in his side. The doctors say he might not make it," she said.

I told her it would be alright but, I knew it was all bad. I told Mrs. Walters that we were going to get some coffee, so I could holler at the homies. We went outside.

"What the fuck happened? I told y'all to watch Pelle," I asked, as I lit my Camel.

"Rock was watching him. You know how Pelle is. He went out to his truck with that bitch to get some head. Money kicked it out there with some chick just to watch out for him," B-Locc said.

"Man, we all left together. Big Q-Ball, Lil Q-Ball, and me rolled together, and Jay Loc, Money and Pelle rolled together. We all rolled the freeway to the city following each other. We got off on Coradell, but Pelle kept going," Rock said.

B- Loc started talking cause he was in the car with Pelle. "Man, we got off the highway to go see if it was cracking at the square. We stopped at the gas station first. When we got to the light at Coradell, D-Money pulled up next to us in his Vet. They started spraying, shooting, at us. They must've had AK's cause they busted for a long time. If Pelle wouldn't have tried to make it all the way to the hood, they would have killed us all. I couldn't even bust back it happened so fast."

"Damn Cuz, my nigga Jay Loc—dead,

"Yeah Man, he got hit in the head four times. His wife, Angel, and my aunt Debra went to I.D. him before you came, man. They left cause it was too hard for them."

We went back inside and got some water and coffee. When we got back on the elevator, I said, "Damn, man! Pelle might not make it. Mrs. Walters said he had a two hour surgery. Who knows where that bitch Stacy lives?"

"I do," said Money.

"B-Locc—you and Money go snatch that bitch up and take her to the ranch. Take the Jag. It has two hand guns and a Tech in the stash. Get what we need to know out of that bitch and then bury her. We'll dig her up and grind that bitch in the meat grinder later."

As we walked off the elevator, we saw the doctor talking to Mrs. Walters and she just broke down.

"No!" we yelled, and kicked the chairs.

"He made it! He made it!" Pam screamed.

So we calmed down. Pam walked toward us and said, "But the doctor said, 'If he makes it through the night, he'll be fine.' He may never walk again. It's a 50/50 chance."

Chapter 3

At 6:00 A.M. we visited Pelle, but he couldn't talk to us, because he was drugged.

"He has another surgery scheduled in six hours. He has a fifty/fifty chance of walking again if it's successful. Moms signed the consent papers. We got some coffee and water for y'all," said Pammy.

We talked to Pelle after Mrs. Walters was done talking to him. We told him to be strong, we were handling it.

Rock stayed with him until the security guard that guarded our parties, arrived to watch Pelle and his family. We told Pammy and Mrs. Walters that we would be back later and not to leave alone. They said that they were staying the night.

"We going to see you at the spot, Rock ... Seven!"

"Alright ... Seven," said Rock

Q-Ball and I had to go meet my White boy, Jeff, who I bought all my guns from. I put an order in for two Ark's, two

MAK-90's, two MAC-11's and a dozen hand guns. He was meeting us at seven on the block. I drove. When I pulled up, Jeff didn't know Q-Balls Beamer, so I rolled down the window.

"Hey Mista, I got those motorcycle parts you need." said Jeff.

Q-Ball and I jumped out and put the stuff in the trunk. I got in Jeff's truck and paid him Ten Grand.

"Damn, Mista," Jeff said.

"What?"

"You going to war with somebody?"

"No, Just staying ready for the war Jeff."

"Alright Mista, stay Black."

"Alright Jeff, stay White." I said, as I smashed off.

We jumped back in Q-Balls Beamer and went to the store at the square. I had two 40 Glocks on me and Q-Ball had two 9's. Q jumped out to get the Remy and blunts. As he was getting back in the car, a black suburban pulled up and someone jumped out of it and ran towards us shooting. I hit the gas, causing the ass end to fish tail out of the lot. Q-Ball busted back. I drove so fast I almost hit the middle lane divider. A bullet shattered the back window as I turned the corner.

I smashed straight to homegirl Lisa's house. That's where we kept our guns. We jumped out and hurried to empty the trunk. Then we went around the corner to the spot. Rock was there. We told him that somebody just tried to smoke us. When B-Locc, Lil Q-Ball and Money came in, we told them.

"I know it was them Greenland niggas," Money said. "Ever since D-Money been home, they been trying to move on us niggas."

"Hey, who drives a black Suburban?" I asked.

"That nigga Chucky from Greenland," said Money.

B-Locc and Lil-Q went and tested the MAC-9's on them busters, while Money put us up on what that bitch Stacy said before they killed her.

"That bitch said D-Money paid her $2,000 to tell him what time Pelle left the party."

"Mista, did anyone see you guys snatch her up?"

"Naw, we caught her going to the store. We talked with her to the car, pointed the heat at her and told her to get in. It was early so the streets was ghost—nobody was out. We sat there watching the Greenland house. D-Money is driving a van. He's moving out of town. That's what that trick said."

B-Locc and Money walked in saying, "Them niggas ain't nowhere in sight, so we shot up they spot and the truck that was parked on the street, to let them know we ain't playing."

My phone rang. "Hello." It was Kelly. "What's up?"

"Mista, I'm at the hospital with Kim and Pamy. They are finished with the other surgery and Pelle is talking."

"Okay, tell him I'll be through in two hours. I got to roll to the house." I hung up.

"Q-Ball … you, Lil Q, and Money watch them Greenland niggas to see what they up to. B-Locc go bury all the money at stop one. That's our emergency get out of town money. Rock I'm gonna pick you up in two hours so we can go check on Pelle. Q, pick up B-Locc and meet us at the hospital. We got to go get our works from the truck stop later. I'm gone. Call Willy at the dealership, and order us six trucks, that way we can roll with each other."

I went home, talked with Raven, showered, changed clothes, and then went to pick up Rock. The L-Boyz were already at the hospital. Pelle could hardly talk because of all the medication he was on. We told him we'd be back tomorrow to holler. Pamy told us that the doctor said that Pelle would walk again after six months of therapy. We were all happy to hear that.

We left the hospital to go get the Blazer and to pick up the trucks from the dealership. After that, we went to the truck stop to pick up our product. When we got there, Lil Q and Money stayed behind in the Cut to watch out as Rock and I went inside to pay for the drugs, and B-Locc and Q-Ball loaded the works in the trunk. Then B-Locc and Q drove the works to the spot, while Lil Q and Money followed them from a distance to see if anybody else followed them.

Rock and I went back to the hospital with In-N-Out burgers for everybody. When we walked in, Kimy was feeding Pelle some soup.

"Where's my burger?" Pelle asked.

"You need vegetable soup for your strength—not burgers," Kimy said.

We laughed.

"My man, that's wifey material right there. Pelle—man— he been here since day one and haven't left your side yet," I said.

"Yeah I know. I'm going to marry her. Life is too short. You never know when you might go. I could be dead right now."

"They tried to take your boy out, my nigga, yeah. They won't get another chance though bro. We on it. You just get well. J-Locc's funeral is Wednesday. We gonna bring you an obituary, cause they say you'll be here for two more weeks. We out."

We left before I got teary eyed. Thoughts were running through my mind of J-Locc being dead. *Next time I see him, he'll be in a casket.*

On our way to cook and bag the product, Rock called Q to get the scoop on the Greenland niggas. B-Locc went to collect the cheddar. While Rock and I were cooking work and bagging pounds, my phone rang.

"Hello, Mista, it's Pamy. The ATF and the Sheriffs are about to raid the house where Quincy's cars are."

"Okay, thanks." The call ended.

"They about to hit!" I yelled.

"Who 'bout to hit?" Rock asked.

"The Feds. Pamy just said."

We kept a barrel filled with acid in the back yard. So we ran the works back there and discarded them. Then we ran back inside to get rid of the shrink wrap, but we were too late.

"Get down or we'll shoot. We have an arrest warrant for Quincy Fuller," The Fed yelled.

They took us in and charged us with sales and manufacturing, even though they found nothing but some cooking ingredients and some shrink-wrap. They said that Quincy was wanted for attempted murder on a minor that was shot sitting on a bus stop during a shootout. They said that his car was identified. I thought, *Damn, more bullshit on top of bullshit.*

I called my lawyer and he posted our bail. We were out in six hours. Our court date was six months off, so we had plenty of time to handle the situation that needed to be dealt with. I had Kelly pick us up because she said that she had something important to tell me in person. I didn't trust my phone or Rocks, so I called Q on Kelly's.

"Yeah, what's good, Kelly?" Q said.

"This not Kelly, Nigga. This Mista."

"Where you at?"

"We sitting watching these suckers. They got two houses over here, ok, but look the Poe-Poe just hit the spot. They took me and Rock to jail."

"WHAT!" Q screamed. "Where y'all at, Mista?"

"We out on bail. They didn't find nothing. They charged us on some manufacturing, but they have a warrant for your arrest. Said some teenager was shot on a bus stop when them fools shot at us. So, you need to get out of town now, while we settle this other shit. Meet us at Chicken and Waffles in Hollywood in twenty-five minutes, alright! ... Seven."

Rock told Kelly to stop at the store for some blunts and cigarettes. I needed one right then—so bad. *There goes kicking the habit.* I thought.

"I got a half up my ass. I wasn't bout to let them find that shit in my pocket," Rock said.

"Boy you crazy," said Kelly.

When Rock went in the gas station's restroom, Kelly said, "Mista, what I wanted to say is ... I haven't had no period. I think I'm pregnant." I was dumb founded; but not mad.

"So, what you want to do? Cause I don't believe in abortion."

"Neither do I, and it's such a relief to hear you say that."

"Look just don't tell Raven. Wait till we have the baby, ok?"

"Yeah, ok, whatever you say. Just as long as you accept my baby."

Rock jumped back into the car.

"Man, I need a cigarette and a blunt to clear my mind." I said.

"Mista you want me to get the vacation house ready for Q-Ball?"

"Naw, Q-Ball going out of town to Jamaica with Lil Q. Call and get tickets ready for them."

We pulled up to Chicken 'n Waffles. We jumped out. Kelly got our table while we talked and I smoked my cigarette. As we ate, we put together a plan and Kelly got the airline tickets.

"B-Locc, Rock, Money and myself will handle this beef while y'all gone. So just lay low. Don't worry. That nigga D-Money ... we gone put Tiff-Tiff on his ass. Money, after she get with his ass, follow them. He thinks with his dick and that's how we gonna catch him."

Rock and B-Locc took Q-Ball and Lil Q to the airport.

Chapter 4

Kelly dropped Money and me off at the ranch. Then she went to get Tiff-Tiff. Tiff was a rat, but she was good at catching niggas. That's where she came in handy. She was chocolate, a bad bitch—only good for giving head and setting a nigga up time after time. I put her on the team long time ago when she put us up on a come-up lick.

We dug up Stacy and grinded her body until there was no trace of it to be found. Afterwards, we went into the Ranch house showered and got dressed. Then we sat and smoked some blunts while I put the map plan down for Money. I told Money to watch and follow D-Money everywhere he went and let Tiff do her magic.

"D-Money gone bite the bait. Just put it out there the right way, alright? And don't show your face for nothing. I know you want to be at the funeral tomorrow, but we need that niggas' head for Jay-Loc and Pelle. You ready, Kelly?"

"Yeah, Mista,"

"Ok, let's roll."

Money and Tiff left together. I walked Kelly to her car, gave her a kiss, jumped in the GMC Sierra, then smashed to the house. I needed some sleep for the funeral tomorrow. I had just went to Raven's father's funeral last month and now I was going to another one.

The funeral was packed with family and friends. Some people went just to say that they were there. It was really sad cause J-Locc, he was only eighteen and had been married a year. But they didn't have any kids. Mrs. Johnson sat on the front row with Jay's father, his lil sister and Linda. Linda was shaking and crying heavily. Angel, J-Locc's wife, tried to jump in the casket with him. We had to restrain her. At the after burial, everyone drank, smoked, and talked about good times with J-Locc. I told Raven she could leave when she was ready and that I was staying so I could handle some business.

I walked Raven to the bullet proof Benz and kissed her good-bye. Then we all went to the spot that we called number two, since spot number one was raided. We weighed, packed and wrapped what needed to be sent out and took it to the workers. We had a good way of moving our works to the states. We had on lock: Colorado, Idaho, Minnesota, Arizona, and Texas. My lady friend, Reeda, had her own shipping and receiving company, so everything made it through. My boy Jaxx would call and say, "The Lakers play at ten." That meant he needed ten more. Or, he would say that the Lakers played at two o'clock, but he missed yesterday's four o'clock game. That meant twenty made it, but forty didn't. Jaxx called B-Locc's phone and said that twenty made it and twenty didn't.

So B-Locc asked him, "How did twenty get through and twenty don't?"

"Nigga, I kill niggas! I don't play with niggas!" Jaxx said.

Then B-Locc started talking crazy. I got wind that he was talking to Jaxx, so I snatched the phone and said, "What's up?" Jaxx started talking crazy so I said, "Nigga lower your voice. This is Mista. What's up?"

He told me the business, and I told him not to trip. The packages all got tracking numbers and that I'd take care of it.

"See you in Miami," I said. Then ended the call.

"Can I kill that fool in Miami?" B-Locc said.

"No, we need him still, right now," I said.

I could tell B-Locc was hot. He is a real killer. Jaxx would pull bullshit moves, like shoot a nigga in the ass, or hit a nigga in the head with the gun, but never killed anybody.

Jaxx had set the meet up for all of the out of town cats for us. We all met in the V.I.P. room at a club in Miami. That way it looked like the meet up was coincidence. We had our meetings there.

I jumped in the Sierra GMC and went to see Reeda.

"Hi Mista, Reeda's in her office," said Reeda's sister-in-law Yola.

I went in and sat down.

"Hey Mista, how's everything?" Reeda asked.

"It's all good Reeda. That's why I'm here. Listen, I need you to check and see what's up on my packages. One of my folks say he only been getting one or two a week instead of the usual four a week. Can't you track them?"

"Yeah, I'll get on it today. You're the third person to tell me that!"

"Okay, Reeda." I said. "Call me and let me know where they been going, and who's signing for them."

I had a plan for Jaxx if he thought he was out smarting me. I had my young homie, Brown Rag, who been waiting to be put on, watch Jaxx out of town. But little did I know that Reeda had been messing with some other cats that were being watched by the Feds. So because of that the Feds were intercepting our shit.

As I was smashing back to the spot, Money hit my phone.

"What's luxury?"

"Mista, just smashing right now! We on. I'm in Arizona. We've been here for four days. D-Money has a house on the westside and a spot on the eastside. I'm in the shoe store across the street from where D-Money and Tiff-Tiff is. They in the 'Hit the Spot' hamburger joint and man I sho want me one of those burgers. I'm going to get one before we leave Arizona. I know Money gonna bite, cause I haven't seen him with no bitch since we been watching him. We're staying at the casino hotel."

"Alright, get B-Locc and me a room. We gonna be out there in 12 hours."

"Alright ... Seven."

I called Rock to tell him what was up. He wanted to go, but he had to handle the business while B-Locc, Money and I was gone. I walked in the house and went in Magazine's toy room and kissed her. Then I went to my bedroom. Raven was watching her favorite movie, *The Nutty Professor,* on T.V.

"Hi, baby"

"Hi, Mista."

I went to the closet grabbed a luggage bag and started packing. I could tell Raven was wondering why cause it wasn't the weekend, so I said. "I got to go to Vegas for business." I gave her a kiss and smashed out in the Jaguar.

I called B-Locc up and told him what Money said. I told him to be ready, I was on my way. When I got there, I honked the horn seven times before Loc came out with his son, Lil Brian. "Hi, Mista." he said.

"Hey, lil man."

I gave him a ten-dollar bill—as always. We went to the hospital to see Pelle before we went to get D-Money. We got to the hospital 15 minutes before the end of visiting hours. We hollered at Pelle, gave him a new cell number to hit us on and we told him we were on our way to get D-Money—we were off.

On the highway we smashed and smoked kush all the way to Arizona. It took us six hours driving nonstop switching drivers every two hours. B-Locc called Money.

"What's luxury?"

"We downstairs meet us in the lobby with our room key,"

"Alright—Seven."

Money came down. We went to our room, dropped our bags, and went to have breakfast.

"Where's Tiff-Tiff?" I asked.

"She with D-Money right now. She going to call us at 7:30. I told her last night that y'all was on your way. It was 6:30 so we had an hour before she was to call. We to showered and smoked while we waited for Tiff to call. About 7:40 Money's phone rang. It was Tiff. Money handed the phone straight to me and I answered.

"Hey, Money," she said.

"This Mista."

"Oh, hey, Mista"

"Where you at Tiff?"

"I'm at the store getting cigarette and blunts."

"Okay, good, can you get him to take you out to eat tonight?"

"Yeah, I should be able to do that."

"Okay Tiff call and let us know where you gonna eat at. We'll be waiting when you come out. There will be a white Lincoln Town Car out front with the keys under the seat and $10,000 in the trunk. Call Kelly and go to where she is in Vegas. She'll give you the address. Use the navigation system to direct you there. You got that?"

"Yeah."

"Make reservation for seven o'clock, we gone be waiting. When you done eating, go to the restroom and call us."

I tossed Money his phone and told him Tiff was going to call us after seven tonight.

"Let's go gamble and find us some pussy," Money said.

While Loc and I was gambling, Money walked up with three Indian bitches. I was talking to Kelly on the phone, so I walked away for a minute.

"Kelly, babe, I'll call you back around four. We'll be there in twelve hours. Tiff will be there in six hours. Listen for her call and give her the directions. Have your shit packed, cause I got some plans for us. Talk to you later."

I never say goodbye cause it's like the end of something. I walked back to where one of the Indian broads was rolling the dice for B-Locc. She hit three grand. B-Locc gave her $300 and we went to the room. We smoked, drank, and flipped them hoes—took turns on all three. After the fuck session, we gave those hoes each $500 to get rid of them. We then fell into a deep coma for a couple of hours. When I woke up, I was like ... "Damn! It's five o'clock. I was supposed to call Kelly at four."

I jumped in the shower, then put on all brown ... same as B-Locc and Money. I called Kelly while we smoked the last spiff that we had rolled, then we each rolled five, smoked and waited for Tiff-Tiff to call. At six o'clock, we put the map plan down while waiting for the call.

Chapter 5

"Look we gone take that buster to the desert where my Uncle Moon use to take me hunting. That's where they buried dead animals that wasn't fit to eat. They bury animals there all the time."

My phone rang.

"Yeah, what's up?"

"Hey, Mista. This Reeda. I got the info of where the packages are going. They're at the Crest Street address in Colorado. The ones that are not there, have not been received cause nobody was there. So, you can pick them up from FedEx and then we can resend them out, Okay?"

"Yeah, Reeda, I just wanted to know if my partner was lying ... saying he wasn't getting them."

Money handed me his phone while it was still ringing.

"Hello."

"Yeah. We at the steak house on Indiana Place. The address is 477 West Indiana Place. I'm in the restroom. We driving a orange 733i BMW. We've been here for fifteen minutes."

"Alright—good work Tiff. Look, take the white Town Car that will be out front. Call Kelly and go straight to Vegas. The On Star is on voice command." I ended the call.

"Let's go get that buster!" I told the crew.

The Map Quest said it was a twenty minute drive, but we got there in fifteen. As we sat in the parking lot smoking, we put the plan down, then got into position. Money was under his Beamer, I was on the side of the building and B-Locc was hiding two cars down from his car. After thirty minutes of waiting, we saw D-Money and Tiff leave the restaurant. As they walked to D-Money's car, I eased from the side of the building and walked behind them slowly. D-Money hit the alarm once they were close to the car. As D-Money stepped around to his door, Money got up from under the car and pointed the MAC-11 dead at him. B-Locc came from around the other car, and I walked up behind D-Money, and said, "What's up D-Money?" His eyes got as big as owls eyes when he saw me.

"You thought we wasn't gonna find you, huh Nigga? See—tricks like you think with their dicks. I put my girl Tiff-Tiff on you. Get on baby ... the car is in front. Get his keys Money, so you can follow us in his car. Walk your bitch ass to that black Avalanche Nigga. If you run, I'm gonna dump six rounds in your back. B-Locc, see if this nigga got a burner on him."

"Naw, he ain't got shit. Bitch ass nigga out here slipping."

Then B-Locc cracked D-Money in the head. I caught him as he fell. We pushed him into the back seat of the truck. I was driving when he came to and I said to him, "D-Money what made you think you could go to war with my clique, kill one of them, and we wouldn't come hard after your ass, huh Nigga?"

B-Locc shoved his gun into D-Money's side and said. "I'm gonna cut your nuts off Nigga."

D-Money was crying as he said, "Mista I don't have no problem with you or your crew. I'm about my money. That was them Greenland niggas, that I sold my Corvette to, that shot up your folks."

"Don't worry we gonna handle them. Just like we did that nigga Stacy—soon too."

I pulled into the desert, drove for ten miles, parked, and then we jumped out of the truck. Money helped B-Locc get D-Money out at gunpoint. I got the shovels, handed one to D-Money, and told him to start digging. After the hole was three or four feet deep, I told him that we were going to bury him alive, and that if he survived, he had better stay gone or he'd be gone. But I was just lying to him.

B-Locc wanted to shoot him in the head like J-Locc had been killed. But I said, "I like to see him suffer and cry like the bitch he is. Wait until the hole is deep enough, then we gonna shoot you in each foot and bury you alive."

Then I shot him in a foot and in a leg. B-Locc shot him in the other foot and leg, and Money shot him in the hand and the arm. D-Money was now lying in the grave that he had dug screaming, "Kill me—don't leave me here like this—kill me, Nigga. I got a half million at my house that I will give you."

"Nigga that's already ours we going to get it after we bury your ass," I said.

We took turns covering him up till we couldn't hear him hollering for us to kill him.

"Nigga you gone die unless you can breathe under dirt. Bitch ass nigga!" I said.

We sat there for about thirty minutes, smoked a spliff and made sure that that nigga couldn't dig his way out. Then we left to drop off the truck to my Uncle Moon's. I told him that he could have it, just get it detailed—twice.

We drove D-Money's Beamer to his house. We pulled on his street and cautiously, checked out all the cars and houses. We then pulled up to the house, hit the remote and went into the crib. I have to give it to that nigga, the crib was tight. He had flat screen TV's in every room, including the kitchen and the bathrooms, even in the laundry room. I made a mental note to hook my shit up like that.

We searched for the paper. I went into the master bedroom. D-Money had a small safe sitting on the side of the computer. I knew it was loaded up with some jewelry, some documents, and a little pocket cash just to throw a nigga off. I went to the closet and searched the walls. I looked behind the picture posters on the walls—nothing. I then walked back to the closet. The floor was covered with shoes. I moved the shoe rack and there it was—the floor safe. B-Locc came in the room. He had found a box in the garage with money in it. D-Money probably was sending it somewhere.

"Nigga you see that safe out there and those watches on the stand?" Money said as I walked in.

"Yeah—fuck that safe! This the one we looking for. Leave that shit alone and don't fuck the place up. That way it will look like ain't nothing missing. If you want one of those watches man, take one, and only one," I said.

"Nigga you can buy your own bling-bling. Get that shit custom made. Let this niggas' money buy it" said B-Locc.

"B-Locc did you see any tools in the garage?" I asked.

"Yeah, it's a tool cabinet and some garden tools in there"

We went in the garage and got the tools. It took us two hours to get the floor safe up. I put all the shoes back in place, we carried the safe out to the car, and threw it in the trunk. We smashed to get the Jaguar and then hit the highway to Vegas. Money and B-Locc drove D-Money's Beamer and I followed them in the Jag. I called Rock to tell him that the business was done and sold to the highest bidder. That meant that the business was handled.

"Have you been to see Pelle?" I asked.

"Yeah, he standing up, but can't walk yet. His legs hurt when he stands up. The doctors said that's good cause he got feelings in his legs"

"Okay, that's good. Is everything cool out there?"

"Yeah, it's all good. I talked to Q-Ball and Lil Q. They out there putting dick to some Dominion bitches."

"All right, I'm gone—Seven!"

The call ended. I called Kelly.

"Hello."

"Hey Mommie, what's up?"

"Nothin—waiting on you. When you coming?"

"I'm on my way. I should be there in two more hours. Did Tiff-Tiff make it yet?"

"Yeah, she been here for about six hours. She in the Jacuzzi."

"Okay, be ready when we get there so we can roll—alright?"

"Yeah," she said, "see you soon."

The highway sign read, Welcome To Nevada. I called Money and told him to follow me to my boy Pepe's chop shop, in the desert, on the outskirts of town. When we pulled in the yard, I told Money to pull to the back and I parked on the side of the office building. I jumped out to greet Pepe. When I walked up, Pepe said, "Hey, Mista what's up my man?" As we hugged and shook hands, I said, "Awl right, just trying to stay above the water. I brought something for you."

Me and B-Locc walked over to the Beamer and got the safe out the trunk.

"I need you to open this for me, and that Beamer is yours. The papers are in the glove compartment. You know how to change it over, right?"

"Oh yeah, don't worry. I got it man," he said.

After Pepe opened the safe, I tossed him a couple of stacks. Then I said, "I'll be ready to go into the business we talked about." We bagged the money and smashed out.

As we pulled up in the driveway, I hit code 777 to get in the gate. B-Locc said, "Nigga how long you had this spot? Nigga, you ain't never took us here as many times we came to Vegas."

"Nigga I got this the last time we came to Vegas. That's where Kelly and me went that day. This our shit— the L-Boyz. Everyone is coming out their pocket with $75,000 each for this."

I parked. We jumped out and walked to the door. Tiff-Tiff opened the door.

"Hey, y'all."

"What's up Tiff? Where Kelly at?"

She was upstairs. I looked around and was like—"Damn! Kelly got taste and class." She had TVs everywhere on the walls, beautiful crystal chandlers, and a sport room with: a pool, a ping pong table, and video game stations in it. In the living room, she put a pearl white piano. I walked up stairs. Kelly was sitting on the edge of the bed.

"I need you to count this paper for me," I said.

"Okay," she replied, "But not until you fuck me!"

I walked up to Kelly. As she set on the edge of the bed, she unzipped my pants and put the log in her mouth—made it triple its size in seconds. It was standing eleven inches tall. I pushed Kelly off the log, pulled her panties to the side, and put the log deep inside. I started slow, then fast, and then a faster pace. Kelly was speaking in tongues. The only thing I could understand was her saying, "Mister!".

After thirty minutes of pounding, we counted the paper. That shit had me tired, so I rolled me a spiff. Kelly kept on counting. I sat back on the lounge couch and lit the spliff. I told Kelly she could no longer smoke cause she was pregnant.

"One Million and Ninety-One Thousand," she said, when she finally stopped counting. In my mind I was like—"That Nigga said a half mill. Damn this is even better. I can give all my niggas a 100 a piece."

"Put $200,000 in one of your purses," I said, "and another $100,000 in two more bags."

I set the $400,000 to the side for the L Boys, then I threw the rest in a Gucci suitcase and handed Kelly $10,000 for counting. Kelly and I jumped in the shower together going for round two. She sucked all the nut out of me. We stepped out the shower and I said, "Kelly go get my bag of clothes out the Jag for me!"

She walked to the closet and opened it, showing me that she had purchased me a wardrobe. I walked over, kissed her forehead, and picked out some white Polo shorts, a yellow and white Polo shirt, and all white Air-Ones. After getting fresher then fresh air, I hopped on the elevator and went down to where Money and B-Locc were. They were outside in the pool skinny dipping with Tiff-Tiff—all laughing and shit. They must have flipped Tiff.

"Yo, B-Locc and Money, let me holla at y'all in the pool house." I walked to the pool house while they put their robes on.

"Yeah, what's up Mista?"

"You niggas must'a flipped Tiff-Tiff?"

"Yeah, you already know," B-Locc said laughing. "Money was telling me how on the way here he was getting head on the road and how good that pussy is. He was fucking her here out in the open, so I put my dick in her mouth. We offered her thizzles too man. That bitch is a cold freak. I didn't know getting your ass licked felt good. That bitch raped me dog!" We all started laughing.

"Look my nigga it's a hundred gee's in here for each of you. It's 200 in the trunk for Rock and Pelle. I got Q's and Lil Q-Baller. Kelly and me going to go to New York, shopping. I'll meet y'all in the city in two days.

"I will call Rock and tell him to catch a plane down here when y'all leave. Let Tiff-Tiff stay here when y'all leave, and only Tiff, Sharie, and Lisa can know about this place. Take everybody else to a hotel. This our safe house.

"We gone start some businesses; a shoe store and a clothing store. It's time to get smart, or we can go down just like all the old heads did. But we gone holler about that when everybody gets here around seven. I'll holler, later!"

Kelly and I jumped in the limo and headed to the airport. It was 9:30 A.M. Our plane was leaving at twelve, so Kelly went and got some snacks, while I called Raven, then Rock.

Chapter 6

We landed in the Atlanta International Airport around twelve in the afternoon. We got our luggage. All that I had in my suitcase was a bag of socks and money. I saw the driver with a sign that said, 'Mista'. We walked over and greeted him

"Hi, I'm Mista."

"Hello, Sir, I will be your driver today. I am pleased to take you wherever you'd like. Hello Madam."

We walked to the Hummer limo. Jeff, the chauffer, opened the door. When we got in Kelly was like, "I never been in a Hummer Limo before babe."

I haven't either, I thought, but I didn't say anything. The line had a fully stocked bar and could probably fit 12 or more people inside. I pulled out my rolled spiff and lit it. While smoking my spiff and drinking Patron, I pressed the button for Jeff.

"Yes Sir!"

"Can you take us to the mall for a shopping square—somewhere everybody goes that's popular? I have an appointment at this address." I handed him the paper though the window that connected to the driver. "Can you get us to the mall quick, then take us to that address? My appointments at three!"

"Yes, sir."

Then he rolled the window back up. I sat next to Kelly and rubbed her thighs. She unzipped my pants and gave me some of the best head I ever had in my life. She knows how to suck a dick. She sucked it, slid her tongue over my dick's head, teased it, and then swallowed everything that it gave. I almost told her I loved her.

"We're here, sir!"

We jumped out and walked up the shopping strip and took in the new atmosphere.

"This is where we gone raise our child," I said. "You cool with that Kelly?"

"Yeah," she replied. "I'm feeling Atlanta!"

"Good cause we meeting Meia, the realtor, after we leave."

Kelly walked into a jewelry store. I walked in behind her. As we looked around, I noticed a bracelet and ring that stood out. They shined like the sun. I called Kelly over to put on the five carat bracelet and the ring—seven carats—my lucky number. You know I had to get it for her. I paid $14,000 for them. I popped open my suitcase and handed the jeweler fourteen stacks.

"Nothing for you, Sir?" he said. He was a good salesman.

"Let me see your watches," I said.

He pulled out ten watches and of course the finest one caught my attention. It was blue brown in yellow—a Cartier Diamond. I took off my rose gold big face Luxury Man watch, and put the new one on. I gave the jeweler ten grand, and told him that he was my new jeweler. He handed me his card and asked if we wanted to personalize our items with engravement or boxes.

When we finished shopping, we had more bags than Kelly, the Chauffer and I could carry. We ordered gumbo and picked it up from a soul food café, then smashed to meet with Meia. Meia said she would ride along with us.

When she got in the car, she said, "I've never been in one of these before."

As we rode, she told us about the area. The houses she showed us were in an upper class area named Buckhead. We pulled in front of one house that looked like the White House. I didn't like it. I wasn't moving to a new neighborhood into a big white house. The next house we drove to was just right. The driveway was made of bridge stone, and the front of the house was brown and gray bridge stone. When we walked inside, I knew it was home, but we did the touring thing anyway. We let Meia tell us all about the house. It was eight years old; built by a ball player who moved and sold the house to a real estate company. It was three stories high, with three bedrooms on each floor. On the top floor was the master bedroom, a gym and a movie room. In the back, there was a lake and a pool with a slide and Jacuzzi attached. We sat out back on the patio lounge chairs, signed papers, ate gumbo, and got the house keys. I told Jeff, the chauffeur, to take Meia back to her office and then come back tomorrow at 7 A.M. I then handed him $500. I planned to find something to drive and see the city early in the morning

I woke up that next morning to Kelly deep throating my log. I laid back and enjoyed feeling the pleasure for about ten minutes, then I pulled Kelly up and put her in the 69 position. I gave her the same pleasure. Her pussy squirted all in my face, at the same time I busted in hers. It felt so good and I was still turned on. My log still stood at its full extension, so I beat her pussy up real good...till I busted up in that thang. Afterwards, I got up and took a shower while Kelly laid there. She was asleep when I came out. I covered her up, and she looked up and smiled.

As I was getting dressed fresher than fresh air, I heard a horn honk. I looked at my watch that I hadn't taken off. It was seven o'clock and Jeff was out front waiting. I woke up Kelly and told her I was going to get us something to drive. I knew that she would be getting the house furnished all day, so I planned on staying gone for a while.

I walked out the front door and told Jeff to take me to a dealership. Jeff pulled up to a B.M.W. dealership and opened the door to let me out. He asked if I wanted him to wait.

"No, thanks for everything," I said.

The Hummer limo must've made quite an impression for me, cause, a fine ass model looking broad walked up to me and said, "Are you shopping for a car?"

"Yes, I am!" I replied,

"Well Sir, follow me. I see that you like the finer things in life."

As I walked behind her, her ass switched from side to side. It made the log jump. She turned around and asked was I looking for a four door, a coupe, or a truck.

"A rag-top coupe, I said.

She smiled and walked over to a black on black rag 650 Coupe, Beemer—like Q Ballers. "Don't y'all make a bigger coupe?" I said.

"Yes, we do have a bigger one on the show room floor. Follow me."

We walked inside the building, and she began her presentation, "This is the 840 Beamer Coupe its top speed is 150 mph, 0-60 in ten seconds, and it's price starts at $100,000!"

"I'll take it," I said.

She turned to face me, gave me a seductive look and smiled.

Then she said, "Step into my office, then we can go for a test drive."

We went into her office and she sat behind her desk. I sat in the chair in front of her.

"What do you do for a living, sir?"

"My name is Mutasur Jenkins, but my friends call me 'Mista'. So you should call me 'Mista'. And your name is?"

"Oh, how so unprofessional of me. My name is Ebony Adams. Nice to meet you Mista!"

"Well I have several very profitable corps, so you can say a C.E.O. of a business."

"How will you be paying for the vehicle, Mista?"

"With my business credit card. I will be paying for it today."

Her eyes got big when she heard that. Then she said, "Well, lets go for that ride."

As I drove, I told her that I was new in town and would like to eat some gumbo. She pointed ahead and I hit the gas. We pulled up in front of the café restaurant. When we walked in, I was shocked. I had never seen so many businesswomen in my life and it looked like they were all having business meetings.

"You must come here all the time!" I said.

"Yeah, I come here at least two or three times out of the week."

The waiter took our order. Ebony order fried catfish and a salad and I ordered oxtails with greens, sweet potatoes, cornbread, and a bucket of gumbo to go.

"How long have you lived here, Miss Adams?"

"Call me Ebony. I lived here for three years after college. I graduated with a bachelors in business. I decided to work as a manager for the dealership because I plan to own my own someday. No woman has ever owned one before, so I'll be the first! I'm from Houston, Texas. That's were my family is. What brings you to Atlanta?"

"Well, I plan on investing in some up and coming businesses. I would love to be an investor in your dealership."

Her eyes got wide like they did earlier—I knew I had her. Our food arrived and we ate. Riding back to the dealership, I said, "I'm serious about investing and helping you own the dealership."

We exchanged numbers and she took the order for a brown, Series eight, four door, with a blue rag top. I would keep the green one for three days and Kelly will pick up the other one. On my way back to the house, I called Raven.

"Hello."

"Hey Mommie, what you doing?"

"Just working out. When you coming home?"

I'll be there tomorrow. I'll call you and tell you what time to pick me up at the airport."

"Ok, love you."

"Love you too!"

 I dialed seven more digits. I hit Rock.

"What's luxury, Cuz?"

"Everything ... I like this spot out here nigga. It's fly."

"Y'all have a ball my niggas, and meet me at the hospital tomorrow at three alright ... seven."

The call ended. I stopped at the store to get some Remy and spiffs, 'cause I planned on fucking Kelly so-o good. *She gone cry tonight before my flight tomorrow at seven.* I thought.

When I walked in the door, I was surprised to see all that Kelly had done in seven hours. She had white carpet laid with brown trimming, a piano sat in the living room, chandeliers were hung, she bought a Sub Zero fridge, and had all the rooms furnished. She did her thang! I was glad, so she couldn't say nothing about me leaving, and I knew she was going to send for her little sister, Roselyn.

"What took you so long to come back?"

"Car shopping, girl."

"What you get?"

"Go see."

"You bought me some gumbo!"

"You know I did."

She went to go look at the car while I rolled my spiff and poured me a glass of Remy.

"You got that for me, Mista?"

"Yeah, and I'm gone have your truck shipped out here tomorrow when I go to the city."

"When you going to the city?"

"Tomorrow morning."

"What am I supposed to do?"

"Go shopping and send for your sister. You probably already have."

"Yeah, I did. She'll be here tomorrow at 9:00 A.M."

"Good, cause my flight leaves at seven in the morning."

While we watched a movie, I smoked my spiff and drank my drink, and Kelly ate gumbo. I rolled over on top of Kelly. I kissed her neck, then her titties, went down to her belly, and on down. I tasted her wetness and then went back up to her lips. After the fourplay, I put my log. deep inside her, and rode the waves like the professional I am. Then, I turned her around and fucked her from behind. The Remy had my dick numb, so I pumped and pumped. Kelly shook, and shook, begging and crying out from the pleasure. After I mashed and smashed up that pussy for an hour, I busted. Then I fell into a deep coma like sleep. I woke up to some bomb ass head. So, as usual, I busted all in Kelly's face. I got up, went to the bathroom, wet a cloth towel with hot water, walked back to the bed, and cleaned Kelly's face. The log was still at full attention, so. I dipped in that pussy from behind. I then took it out, and smashed it into her ass, and then fucked her ass while playing with her clit. She hollered my name for about ten minutes. Then busted all over my fingers as she shook in convulsions.

Afterwards, I jumped up and hit the shower. I knew she would be straight for a least a week and I planned on being gone that long. After getting fresher then fresh air, I woke up Kelly so she could drop me off at the airport.

"When you gonna be back, Mista?" she asked.

"When I finish handling my business," I replied, "most likely a day or two."

I leaned over to kiss her lips and said, "I'll see you later." I never say goodbye to anyone because it's like I'm ending something.

Before boarding my first-class flight, I called Raven and told her to be at the airport at 9:30 when my flight arrived. When I walked through the terminal of the airport, I saw Raven and she looked sexy as ever. She knew how to turn me on. She had on white stretch pants with a Gucci belt wrapped around her waist. The print in the stretch pants was so phat, and she wore a Gucci tank top that showed off her sexy titties and nipples. She looked so good that the log was almost standing at attention.

"Hey Mommie," I said, giving her a long tongue kiss. Then I asked.

"Where's my daughter, Magazine."

"She's with my momma. You know since my daddy died mom needs somebody to be with her at that house."

Raven drove to Tony's, a café that we always went to eat at when we were out together. As we ate, I saw that Raven was ready to get dicked down by the log. The lust and horniness was in her eyes. So when I popped my vitamins, I also popped a blue X-pill. The blue ones had you fucking for hours. On the way to the house, I lit a spliff that took it to the next level. Then I hit seven digits to call Rock and see if they left yet.

"What's luxury, Cuzz?" I asked.

"All the finer things." he said.

Chapter 7

"When y'all gonna be in the city?"

"I'm with wifey. We on the highway, headed to the house. Alright, seven," I said, and we hung up.

At home I poured me a glass of Remy and Moet. I then walked into the bedroom only to find Raven on our bed completely naked. I swallowed my drink and walked to the bed. I took off my shoes and shirt and Raven unbuttoned my pants. We were both asshole naked. Raven is a cold love-making freak in the bedroom, behind closed doors. She reached over and grabbed some chocolate strawberry oil. She rubbed it all over my body, and I rubbed it all over her tits, neck, stomach, and thighs. We sucked each other until our tongues hurt. Then I put my log in her river. I called Raven's pussy that because she got as wet as a wild river. I fucked Raven every which way ... standing up, lying flat, on top of her, froggy, doggy and even loggy; that's when she laid on her side and I entered her from behind. Afterwards, we both fell in a coma like sleep.

When I woke up it was two o'clock. I jumped up and showered. Then I put on everything black: 501's, Avrex sweater, socks, watch, black diamond pinky ring, hat, and the Jays. I then smashed it to the city. Pelle was getting out of the hospital today. All The L-Boyz had to be there for him. As I walked into Pelle's hospital room, I could hear his uncle Pete's loud drunk ass mouth and everybody else talking.

"Mista, I know you got the niggas who shot my nephew," Uncle P said when he saw me.

I didn't say a word to him. I just gave Uncle P "the look".

"What's up everybody?" I said.

Pelle told me that he was going to marry Kim, and that his Uncle P and his girlfriend were going to stay with them while he healed. I told Pelle that I would stop through once a week to check on him. Pelle was only able to walk for a couple of minutes at a time, so for now he still needed the use of a wheel chair. He was told that after a few weeks of physical therapy, he should be walking well again. As I wheeled him out of the hospital, I let him know about the house in Vegas, that the L-Boyz were on their way and that I had a few thousand for him. The L-Boyz pulled up as I was helping Pelle into the truck. We all went to Pelle's house to party. Pammy did not stay long, so when she left, I walked her to her car and thanked her for giving us the heads up on the raid.

"You know that you are like my brother Mista. You and Pelle are good men. Y'all chose your own paths, but it's time to go legit before it's too late. I told Pelle the same thing. I know what y'all do."

"We doing just that sis," I said.

I gave her a hug and then I turned and walked back into the house. I explained to the L-Boyz that we now had a legitimate status in society because we owned a burger stand, a customs car shop and a clothing store that would soon feature our own clothing line. Pelle told me that Pammy was going to hit the Greenland hood with indictments. We all slept at Pelle's that night.

The next morning, we got busy. B-Locc went to collect paper, I met with Oscar, our plug, and Rock, Money, and one of the workers named Black Hawk got our packages at Fed-Ex. When Rock, Money, and Black Hawk got in the car with the works, the Feds surrounded it from all directions. They placed them all under arrest. B-Locc and I were at the customs shop checking on the place when I got the call from Raven. She told me that Rock, Money, and Black were in the Feds and they were charged with conspiracy, trafficking, and money laundering. She said they needed a lawyer to bail them out. I told Raven to call Mr. Spartacus and have him go see them. Then I ended the call.

"Fuck, Cuzz." I yelled, kicked and dented my freshly painted Benz. Let's roll," I said to B-Locc while he was talking on the phone.

He hung up. He said that he was talking to his wife, Sammy, who told him what Raven had just told me. I hit the seven digits and called Reeda's business. Yola answered.

"Can I speak to Reeda, Yola? This Mista!"

"The police raided her today and took Reeda to jail, Mista."

"What?" I said, and hung up.

"We gotta get out of town, cause they waiting to catch us." I said to B-Locc.

B-Locc and I left and got a room that I paid a prostitute to put in her name. We sat in the room and smoked spiffs back-to-back and drank.

"We need that buried money. I got a plan. Tomorrow's Tuesday; trash day. You'll dress up like a trash collector and we'll pay the trashmen to let you ride along and pick up the trash at the house. I'm gonna get a gas company uniform and go in the backyard and dig up the money and put it in the trash. It's under the barbeque grill, right?"

"Yeah."

We got our costumes from a costume shop in Hollywood and waited until morning. I couldn't sleep. I probably slept for three hours. The next morning we put our plan to work. I rented a white truck and put a gas company sticker on it. I then hit seven digits to put Pelle down on the news. I told him to lay low and move down South somewhere. Then I hung up. I dropped B-Locc off three blocks away from the spot in the hood where we knew a trash man, and he gladly accepted the two grand to help us. I then parked six houses away from the spot and walked to the side of each house pretending to make notes; like I saw gas workers do. I was really checking out the cars on the block. When I got two houses down I saw them, the Feds, parked across the street, sitting in a brand-new blue Tahoe with super tinted windows.

I walked to the spot and went into the side back gate. Beauty, our Pit Bull, walked towards me. "Hey Beauty," I said. She walked up to me, got my scent and licked my hand. I grabbed the shovel that I had my lil' homie next door put on his side of the gate, and went straight to work. I pulled the five duffle bags of money up just as I heard the trash truck coming. I threw the bags in trash cans and walked through the gate out of the yard, writing on the note pad. I walked back to the parked truck, pulled around the corner, and waited for B-Locc. The trash truck pulled around the corner ten minutes later. When they got to where I was parked, B-Locc jumped out with the five bags, got in the truck and then we smashed off. I returned the truck and walked across the street where Lisa left another rental for us. We then smashed to the safe house in Vegas. Once there, B-Locc and I got pissy drunk. I told B-Locc that I was going out of town to put some business shit down that would make us legitimate millions and that we needed some new identities.

The next day, I went to see my boy PePe, who owned me a favor. He made us new ID's and social security cards. Later that night I left B-Locc $70,000 and hit the highway. We had phones that we would only talk to each other on and everybody else a different one. On the highway, I hit seven digits and called Raven.

"Hey babe."

"Hey Mista. Why you didn't come home?"

"Cause I got to lay low right now. The Feds are waiting to catch me there. I know it. I got to call Mr. Spartacus to see if I'm indicted with Rock and them. He told me to give him a day. So, let me call him, love you."

I hung up and hit seven more digits.

"Hello."

"Yeah Spartacus, this Mista. What have you heard?"

"Well Mista ... You, Matasuar Jenkins, Shapell Walters and Kelly Spells are all on the indictment. You are on top and facing 20 years to life. Everyone else is facing 10 years for conspiracy. If you want to turn yourself in, come to my office and I'll have them pick you up here."

"I'm not turning myself in, Spartacus. When do they go to court and do they have a bail?"

"Well, they are due back in court in four months and the bail hearing is in a month; but, because they are calling you guys a notorious street gang and drug traffickers, I don't think they will get bail."

"Alright, Spartacus, I'll be in touch."

I hung up. It felt like the weight of the world was on my shoulders. I lit a Camel — non-filter — smoked that, then lit, and smoked a spiff.

$$\$$$

Welcome To Alabama the sign read. I exited the highway, returned the rental car, and called a cab. The cab dropped me off in front of a house that no one knew about. Raven and the L-Boyz didn't even know about it. I got the house just in case something big happened. The yard needed to be cut badly and the inside was dusty as hell. So, I cleaned up the place, cut the grass, and cleaned the SS Impala and SS truck that sat in the yard. I smoked me a spiff after that and then went to bed and fell into a coma like sleep.

I woke up around seven that night, ordered a pizza, and put my plan together to get Ebony on my team to clean the dirty money. After I ate, I went outside and buried some of the money and then I put some of it in the wall. I plastered the wall back up, then I smoked a spiff. I called Kelly and told her that she was on the indictment list. I told her that I would be there in two days, even though I was only hours away. I hung up.

The next morning, I showered and put on an army uniform. I told the neighbors that I was in the military and stayed on the army base. I called for a cab and was dropped off at a car rental place. I rented a 300 Chrysler and then I headed to Atlanta to put the "Ebony" plan into action. When I got to Atlanta, I got a presidential suite in a hotel because they are safes in them. I didn't want to carry a half million dollars on me. After jumping in and out of the shower, I was fresher that fresh air. I put on an Armani suit, a Kenneth Cole button down shirt, with some blue gators. I crushed some ecstasy pills, put them in an ice cube tray, then in the mini fridge. After that I headed out to see Ebony. Hitting the seven digits, I called Ebony.

"Fancy Cars, this is Ebony Adams. How may I help you?" she answered.

"Well you can start by telling me you are ready to start your own dealership and are resigning."

"Hi, Mista!"

"Hey, how are you today?"

"I'm fine and you?"

"I'm fine too. I just got back in town and wanted to talk to you about the dealership. Have you called and talked to the bankers and car distributors?"

"Yes, I have and I need a million dollars up front for them to back me. I found a lot near the shopping malls. I can get it for $300 thousand with 150 down."

"I'm out front. Go let your boss know that you won't be working there anymore as of right now and we can get this business rolling. Let's go celebrate."

Ebony came walking out with her suitcase. I was sitting on the hood of the Chrysler. She walked up with a glow in her eyes. I hugged her and said, "Let's go eat and party." We went to the same café that we went to the day I met her. As we ate, I asked her what name did she have in mind for the dealership.

"Mr. and Mrs. Benz's, I want to sell Benz's."

"You crazy, but the name sound good," I said.

We left and went to purchase the lot. After Ebony talked with the bankers and made appointments, we went to party at the strip club. Ebony liked Cristal champagne, so I ordered her two bottles of Moet and for my taste I ordered Remy, plus two shots of Patron for the both of us. When Ebony went to the restroom, I popped a pill and snorted some White Girl. I planned on breaking Ebony in and making her my bitch. After four shots of Patron each, we were both ready to go.

We went back to my suite. I poured us a glass of Champagne and put four ice cubes, that had the letter E in them, in each of our glasses. We got into the Jacuzzi and talked about everything. Ebony started dancing and grinding up against me to a R. Kelly song. By this time the pills started working. I picked her up and set her on the edge of the Jacuzzi and pulled off her thongs. Then I licked and sucked on her pearl tongue till she shook and moaned. Then I licked her asshole and sucked on her clit.

"Oh, my God, oh, my God, oo-wo-wee, yes, ooh wee." She moaned.

When she became so excited that she couldn't hold herself up on the edge of the Jacuzzi or above the water, I picked her up and carried her into the shower. I knew that being on Ecstasy and with so much drink in our systems we needed to stay wet and cool, so I put the water temperature on just above warm. I made it cool and just right for us. We got in and I sucked every bit of water off her tits, stomach, and ass checks. After that, we walked to the bed soaking wet and I put the log in deep. Her eyes got big when she felt the log. She put her hand down there to make sure I wasn't fucking her with something else. I rocked the boat and rode the wetness like the pro that I am. The X and the powder had my dick numb, so I pounded that pussy viciously. She begged me to stop, but I had to give her the anthem log treatment. I started pounding harder screaming. "Give it to me! Give it to me!" Then I flipped her over and put the log deep in her ass, while playing with her clitoris. She tried to run, but that was not happening. I mounted on top of that thing as she cried in pleasure. I then flipped her back over and nutted in her pussy.

She fell right to sleep after that three-hour sextion. Ebony laid there naked looking sexy as hell, with her golden blond hair, and butterscotch skin. With all the things that I had on my mind, plus the X, and the stiff log, I couldn't sleep. So I jacked off while I looked at Ebony sleep. I squirted cum all over her ass checks and her back as she slept on her stomach and I left it there. I woke up that morning after sleeping for two hours. I hopped up, showered, and got fresher than fresh air. I ordered room service: steak, eggs and hash browns for Ebony, two boiled eggs for me and orange juice for both of us.

I went to purchase her an outfit from the clothing store down stairs. I got her a nice pair of Phat Pharm jeans, a satan royal blue shirt to match, and blue denim jeans. I went back upstairs to wake her, so that she could shower before breakfast. She came out of the bathroom looking like the super model that she could be. She sat in front of her breakfast, as I drank her orange juice. Before I could say anything, she said. "Where have you been all my life." Then she asked me if I was married and wanted to know where did we go from there. I told her about Raven and Kelly and that neither one of them had the potential to be my wife— but she did. I told her that I wanted her from the very start. I knew I had her right where I wanted her. I told her about my childhood and she told me about hers. We talked for over an hour. I told her everything except about the illegal things and the indictment against me. We made plans to find a house and move in together after I got back from my business trip and she started the process of getting the dealership up and running. I dropped her off at her car, which was still parked at her job, so she could clean out her office. I went to the house with Kelly dressed like I was at a business meeting.

$$\$$$

Three Months Later

I was sitting in front of the 70-inch TV screen at the house that Ebony and I had together and decided to call Raven. She answered the phone crying.

"What, what's up Raven ... baby!" I screamed.

"They came here and raided this morning. They busted up the walls and dug the back yard up, and they took your old school cars that's in your name. I don't know what to do!"

"Look Raven! Sell the house and move to Atlanta, ok? I'll give you a call with the house alarm code. Be out there by then." I hung up. "Fuck!," I said.

The house code was seven spelled backwards. That meant that I would call Raven in seven days. I jumped up and called out to Ebony that I had to go to Vegas for a meeting. I got in the 600 Benz, a car from the dealership company, and started the drive to the spot in Alabama so that I could think and talk with Pammy. I needed to know if Pelle was hit too. While on the highway, I called B-Locc using a throw away phone that couldn't be traced or tapped.

"Hello Locc."

"What's Luxury, my nigga?"

"You straight?"

"Yeah, Mista, I'm just laying low waiting on Q-Baller and Lil Q to get here. They said. they will lay low out here with me."

"Alright my nigga, y'all lay low homie ... Seven."

I hung up. Then dialed seven more digits and called Mr. Spartacus.

"Hello Mr. Spartacus, this Mista. What's going on with the case and my folks?"

"Well Mista, they have picked up several others for conspiracy related to the case. A Mr. Jesse Fairs, aka Jaz, Cory Lays, aka Cowboy, Maurice Gibbs, aka Murder, Kevin Jenkins, aka Wood, and Michael Thomas, aka Big Mike.

The bail hearing is next week. I'll let you know that day if there is any success on getting bail."

"Ok, thanks Mr. Spartacus."

I stopped at the rental place to leave the Benz and then caught a cab to the house. I wanted to keep a low profile in this neighborhood so I changed into my military outfit. I drove up to the spot and pulled up to the curb in front of the house. The grass was so high it needed to be cut, so I did what I did every time I went there. I cut the grass and dusted and cleaned the inside the house. I never ordered lawn service because I didn't want anyone to notice that the place stayed empty and everything in it was worth some money. After that I showered, and then laid back and smoked a spliff. Then I hit seven digits and called Pelle.

"What's luxury, Cuz?" I spit.

"Just maxing out Nigga. Trying to get these legs one hundred again."

"That's right. Did you do that yet?"

"Yea, we out in two week. I had a private room made. Everybody know to turn their tv's on and watch the news!"

That meant all workers knew to shut down shop and watch for the police.

"They raided the house. Raven is smashing too. I'll hit you in a couple weeks alright? ... Seven."

The call ended. I sat back on the Dallas Cowboy couch that I specially ordered. I wondered if I should just pack up and leave with all the money that I had. I dropped that thought. My mind turned to the million dollar deal I was about to make from the dealership.

$

Four Months Passed

I was going and coming as I pleased. Pelle moved to Alabama. Raven moved to Atlanta. Kelly was five months pregnant and Ebony was two. It was easy keeping all three of them sexually satisfied and mentally tamed. I stayed two days a week with Raven using the excuse that I didn't want to bring any heat to the house. With Kelly I did whatever I wanted, and I stayed with Ebony three days a week, out for business.

Ebony and I got married in the Bahamas and then went to meet each other parents. Ebony's pops was real cool. He was a high school coach and her mom was still gorgeous. She looked just like Ebony. To be forty-four, her body was tight, she was a principle of a junior high school. We had dinner with her parents and stayed the night. The next day her parents drove us to the airport to catch a midnight flight to my grandmother's home that my mom now lived in. She moved in after her mom passed away seven years earlier, but I still call the place 'Grannies' House'. Moms asked Ebony a million questions and she gave me the eye, because she knew that I was still with Raven, and that Kelly was pregnant — but Moms would ride with her son, the black superman, to the fullest. That's why I did anything for my momma. While Ebony and Moms talked, I walked to the dining room and hit seven digits.

"What's luxury, Cuz?"

"Did Q-Baller and Lil Q-Ball get there?"

"Yea, they here. They got those fake ID's and they been out every day on the strip partying and gambling. I'm just lounging and working off this gut I got from sitting around."

"Nigga that's what the pool is for," I said, then I ended the call.

My phone began to play Jay-Z's song, "Go Getta", so I answered it.

"Yeah, Hello!"

"Hey Mista, this is Mr. Spartacus. There will be no bail. They are offering plea agreements to everyone: ten years to life for aka Rock, Young Money, Black Hawk, Reeda. and also everyone else. They are all signing their deals, because there is no beating trial and loosing means getting thirty years or life."

"Okay, thanks Mr. Spartacus."

The call ended.

Chapter 8

Ebony and I drove back to Atlanta that following morning after visiting moms. I laid around the house all that day and night. Ebony slept while I watched "America's Most Wanted" and my worst fear came true. There I was in a picture with the L-Boyz when we were all seventeen. I sat there dump-founded. I knew then that I had to cut off my braids and mustache. I jumped up and got the scissors and razor and cut off all the hair on my head and my face.

I looked in the mirror and thought *You still handsome and fresh.* I lit a Camel as I walked downstairs to the basement and called B-Locc.

"Hello," Tiff answered.

"Yeah ... where's B-Locc and them niggas at, and who else is there?"

"B-Locc, Q-Baller, and Lil Q-Baller they in the lounge room watching basketball. It's only Mary, Lisa and me here."

"Take the phone to B-Locc."

"What's Luxury Cuz?" B-Locc spit.

"Look Loc, we on "Americas Most Wanted" Nigga. Everybody took ten years and we need to turn ourselves in soon, so lay low. No more going out partying for y'all. We got the businesses plus the dealership to keep us good till we get out. I'm gone. I got to call Pammy and Pelle, seven!"

The call ended and I lit another Camel. I was smoking back to back. I made me a shot of Remy XO—then another. I got dressed and went to see Raven and my daughter, Magazine. After kissing my daughter on the forehead, I had a talk with Raven. I told her I was on my way to jail to serve some years, but I would do about ten or eight years in all. She started crying then dried her eyes, took off my shirt and gave me a hot wax massage. She always knew how to relieve my stress. She slowly undressed in front of me with her back turned to me. She pulled down her pants and touched her toes repeatedly in her sports panties. Then she exposed her breast. She turned around, squatted down and unbuckled my belt. She took off my pants, and my Ralph Lauren boxer briefs and she put my warm log in her mouth, while massaging my balls.

"Damn! Raven — I love you," I said.

After putting the log down and standing it up again, she sat on it and grinded it.

"I love this big dick. I love you," she whispered in my ear. After letting her work hard, I went to work. I stood and walked her all over our massive bedroom. I put her back to every wall, as the log hit every wall inside her. I laid her down on the fox skin rug that we had on the floor and I rode the wild river with the log till her pussy exploded like Niagara Falls. Then I laid there inside her till that position hurt.

The following morning the Fed's hit the house in Vegas. Q-Baller felt like he was going to get life with the attempted murder and conspiracy charges the Fed's had against him, so he started blasting and got himself killed. Everybody else surrender. After hearing that news from Pammy, I hung up and lit another Camel. I told Kelly that I would sign a deal, if the Feds would let her off. I jumped in my Bentley and smashed off to the smoke shop to get some spliffs and a carton of Camels. When I walked out of the store, I saw a black Hummer parked behind my car with all four doors open. Four men in all black surrounded me. My heart started beating fast. I was thinking ... *This is it.* To my surprise they never yelled—"Freeze!" ... "Put your hands up!" or ... "You're under arrest!" I stood there stunned till one of the men said.

"Oscar wants to see you, Mista. Come with us. Give me your keys. I'll drive your car."

I got in the Hummer with the three men. We rode in silence. We went to a warehouse about thirty minutes out of town. I was escorted through the front entrance and upstairs to Oscar's office. He was sitting at his desk with two high heeled naked women on each side of him. The two women walked out and two of the men stood on each side of me and the other next to Oscar.

"Mista, long time no see. You don't call, neither do you pay me my money. You owe me $2 million. I began to worry that you forgot about who put money in your pocket!" Oscar said.

"Look, Oscar. Me and my homies are all indicted by the Feds. Rock, B-Locc, and everybody else in my click, they all in jail. Me and Pelle are on the run. That's why you haven't seen or heard from me, but I have your payment. You know how I get down Oscar. I just didn't want to bring the heat on you! Shit is fucked up for me right now. My whole operation is shut down."

"Well, I see you still doing very good for yourself with the business and the Mr. and Mrs. Benz dealership."

"You sho do your homework Oscar. Don't you?"

"Yes, Mista, or else I would be indicted with you. I have close eyes on everyone I deal with, and my hand is in the right people's pocket. I like what you have done, Mista. I have a few federal judges on the payroll. Maybe — I'll be able to get you and Pelle off the indictment, but everybody else that's in jail is already stuck. You owe me $2 million. I do not want the money. I want you to use it to open another dealership in California so I can wash dirty money. This will be better work for you and very appreciated by me and my family. Do you think you can do this Mista?"

"Yeah Oscar — with ease, but I need not to be on the run no more, or any of my folks that's not in jail."

I said that so that Kelly could be off the hook.

"Don't worry, Mista. I'll take care of that. Have the dealership opened in two months. I have a large shipment of cash coming in then. Hector, give Mista a phone."

Hector handed me a phone from a shopping bag.

"Mista, that phone is only for you to contact me or me to contact you. It cannot be tapped or traced. I'll be in touch with you in two months to give you instructions. See you, Mista."

Two of Oscar's men escorted me out of the building and one of them handed me my keys. I jumped in the car and smashed the long road back to Kelly's and my house. I told her everything, how we will be alright, and what Oscar said about the case getting dropped against me. She really needed to hear that. Kelly was carrying my son and I didn't want anything stressful to jeopardize his health.

I woke up to some bum skully and good pregnant pussy. I showered and got fresher than fresh air. I rode on the highway to the "Luxury Fits" clothing store that we owned. Then I called Pammy.

"Hello."

"Hey Pammy, how are you?"

"I'm fine, Mista. How you holding up?"

"Just taking it day by day sis."

"How was the funeral? Did anyone take pictures?"

"Yeah, Quincy's cousin Paula took pictures. I know the Feds were there taking pictures and waiting for y'all to arrive."

"Yeah, I know. Tell Pelle that I said, 'What's up?', and that we will soon be ok."

"How do you figure that Mista?"

"You both need to get yourselves ready to do some time in jail or run for the rest of your lives. I hate it for y'all, but y'all chose the life"

"Yeah, you right Pammy. You know you are the only way to send word to Pelle. Thank you for always being there for us. Talk to you later Pammy."

She didn't need to know that the indictment would soon be squashed. Later that night I talked with Ebony over dinner. I let her know that I wanted to open a dealership in California.

"I thought you hated California," she said.

That's what I told her when she wanted to go there and shop on Rodeo Dr. in Beverly Hills.

"Well I don't hate money or opportunities so, Cali here we come. We will buy a condo, so that when we are there, we have a place to stay. This next one will be a Chevy dealership though. I will call it 'Mash Motors and Luxury Cars'.

"Ok, Mista. I'll call Karl and see if he can get us a lot."

"Make sure you tell him somewhere in the suburbs. Nowhere in the Los Angeles area."

"Okay," she said.

$

Two years passed like nothing. Both of the dealerships were bringing in paper. Plus, every month the $400,000 that went into the business account would just get wrote out as cars sold. Pelle now walked with only a slight limp. The cleaners and the burger stands were washing all the money that the young homies brung in from the spots in the hood. Kelly had my son and we named him Matasur Jr. Ebony had a little girl. We named her Emani.

I was leaning back in the leather recliner behind my cherry oakwood desk, smoking my cigar when my secretary, Sherry, buzzed me.

"I have a call from Lil Q on line two."

"Hello."

"What's luxury, cuz?"

"Just living. Y'all straight? Got enough paper on your accounts."

"Yeah, I'm good."

I had Mona, the homegirl, put four thousand on the L-Boyz books every two months.

"I was just calling to spit a few words with you and the family. Like I do every month on the seventh."

"Everybody straight. We just waiting on y'all to finish walking down the time and come live this luxury life my nigga. Everybody straight in there?"

"Yeah, Rock is cool. Yung Money straight. Black is in a State Prison now for that stabbing. Look they just called yard movement. I'll hit you next month on the same day, seven."

The call ended.

Chapter 9

Three years passed since Pelle was shot and Pammy had the Greenland hood indicted. Big Chucky was railroaded and was given twenty years for being in front of a house that had dope and guns in it. There was no proof shown that he lived there. There were no bills or mail addressed to him and nothing with his prints on it was found anywhere in the house. His lawyer has been appealing his case since he was convicted.

Each night, Correction Officer Barbara Mayford counted the inmates and passed out mail to the those that missed mail call earlier because they were either working or on the yard. Charlie Baits, aka Big Chucky, always received stock books and stock holder mail. Officer Mayford was interested in stocks and always stopped and talked to Big Chucky for a few minutes each night. He was the only prisoner she knew that received mail about stocks. After giving Big Chucky his mail for over a year, Officer Mayford told Chucky that she became a Federal Correction Officer at the Federal Bureau of Prison in Beaumont Texas after she lost all her money in the stock market. She told Chucky that she had inherited $500,000 from her parents who were killed returning from a vacation trip, and she invested it all in the stock market, and lost everything because she did not fully know how the stock market game worked. Chucky told her how he was convicted without any evidence or proof of him being in the house and that he was waiting to win his appeal sooner or later.

One month, Officer Mayford worked double shifts every day, meanwhile Chucky didn't go to the yard for one week. His lawyer had filed another motion and Chucky only went to the library and back to his cell to study his case and the appeal.

One day, during this time, Officer Mayford called yard movement. Everyone that wanted to go to the yard, the music room, watch TV or use the phone left their units. Ms. Mayford walked the unit to see if anyone was left that wanted to leave their cells. Chucky noticed that when she passed his cell that she did not acknowledge him with even a simple,"Mr. Baits". He noticed that she had been working day and night for a month and he sensed that something was wrong. *It must be her man.* He thought. He stood near the cell door which was cracked open and waited for her to pass back by him on her way out.

"How's your day Ms. Mayford? I noticed that you have been working double shifts lately," he said, when she passed. She stopped and looked at him as if to say 'Don't speak to me like that.'

"Damn, is everything okay, Ms. Mayford?" He said.

She thought about how she always spoke to him and felt that just because she was in debt with bills, it wasn't his fault.

"I'm just tired," she said.

"You should be, as much as you been working."

"Well that's the only way to pay the bills off with the debt that I'm in," she said, with watery eyes.

"Look Officer Mayford you are the only one who treats a brother or anyone in here like a human being. I consider you a good person and a friend. Under these circumstances we've been seeing and talking to each other for over a year. I respect you so if there's anything I can say or do to brighten your day for just a minute, I would do it."

She stood there for a second and thought to herself, *Who do he think he running game on?*, but said, "Thank you, but the only thing that can get me to brighten up right now is $10,000 that I owe in taxes," and she walked off.

Chucky left his cell and made a phone call to his accountant and investor, Janett. They went to community college together. Janett majored in Accounting and Investment and Chucky in Business and Management. They became good friends after Chucky offered her a ride one rainy day when her car wouldn't start. Later in the friendship, he loaned her some of his drug money to start her accounting and investment business. He wanted to fuck Janett because she was half Japanese and Black, but he kept it strictly business. He gave Janett instructions to give Ms. Mayford $20,000 for a business loan. He told Janett not to question the lady about the business.

Later that evening when Officer Mayford passed mail to the inmates that missed mail call, which Chucky had none because he had gotten his earlier, he stopped her and handed her a note that read, "*Read me when you get off work*", at the top of it. She read the top and looked at him for a second and then put it in her pocket and walked away.

That night after work Officer Mayford ate baked chicken, rice, and broccoli, and then took a hot bath. She was sitting on her bed fantasizing about Big Chucky's chiseled body lying on top of her, when she remembered the note in her uniform. She got up and went to her dirty clothes basket, pulled the note from her pants and read it. The note said,

Hello Ms. Mayford,

Since I don't know your first name.

Like I said earlier, you are a good person and a friend to me. Do you consider me a friend? I know I'm in prison, but you don't treat me like that.

Well, I'm writing this letter cause you said you needed $10,000. Since you are a friend, I called my accountant, Janett Jergens, and told her a place to meet you. She will bring you the money. It's not dirty money. I earned it through various investments, plus I'm a silent owner in her accounting and investment company. Her number is (717) 555-7767. Ask for Janett. Tell her you're Ms. Mayford. She will know what to do. Have a good night Ms. Mayford. Hope this relieves your stress. Pay your bill.

Dumfounded she laid there and thought to herself that not anyone in her family, co-workers or friends, would lend her that type of money. She wasn't gonna call Janett, but changed her mind and first thing the next morning she was on the phone setting up the meeting. She got dressed, called off from work, and went to meet Janett at a Starbuck's coffee shop. They had coffee. Janett told her, she was a Certified Public Account and offered her any help that she needed. Janett handed her a business card and a certified check signed over from Jergen's Professional Accounting Inc. for the amount of $20,000. Officer Mayford's eyes almost popped out of her eye sockets when she looked at the check. Officer Mayford and Janett shook hands and departed.

Officer Mayford went straight to her credit union and deposited the check. Then she wrote a check for her unpaid house taxes and $1,200 for her two months back car note. She felt so good at home for the first time in a very long time. She turned on the water in the tub for a soothing bubble bath. The water felt so good, all she could think about was Chucky. He was her hero. She closed her eyes and immediately she saw his face, hard body, and eyes, and she felt the compassionate attraction she didn't want to admit they shared. Afterwards, she went shopping at the fish market. She then went home and made her favorite dish: lemon and orange curry salmon with butter lobster. She cleaned her kitchen, showered, and then laid in her bed and sipped on a glass of Merlot. She quickly fell to sleep.

The dream she had woke her up with soaking wet panties. It was about Chucky. He had her bent over in the mop room at the prison, fucking her. Her pussy was so hot and wet, that she grabbed her dildo from the drawer, took off everything, sucked on her tities, and fucked herself while calling out Chucky's name saying, "Oooh Chucky! Charlie, my hero! Oooh yes, Chucky, Chucky," till she exploded and fell in a coma like sleep. The next morning, she thought, *I slept better than I have in years.*

On her way to work, she couldn't stop thinking of Chucky and how she wanted to give him some pussy. She had written a note and planned on giving it to him later that night. Officer Mayford, walked the unit passing out the mail after her inmate count. When she went to Chucky's cell she slid him his mail and note under the door. Since there was not a book she had no need to open the cell. She wrote on top of the note, 'Read me before you go to sleep tonight'. Chucky looked through his mail, read the letter from his sons and then the one from Officer Mayford. It said:

To a friend
From your friend Barbara

I don't know how to thank you. First, let me say you are a blessing and I will pay you back soon. I don't know how or what I can do for you to show my appreciation. But I have something in mind and I hope that you will win your appeal so that I can cook you a home cooked meal. I know it's been a while since you had one!

P.S.
Your friend

Chapter 10

Chucky laughed to himself. He knew that he just opened a door to a whole lot of opportunities. Over the next few weeks, Chucky and Barbara wrote each other notes that soon turned to love notes and sexual poems. One afternoon, after doing his usual pull-ups, dips, and push up sets, Chucky was walking the track and listening to his I-pod that Barbara had given him from the outs. The I-Pod was loaded with his favorite songs by Tupac. He was walking the track and singing along with the words.

> *Cause you ain't never had a friend like me,*
> *I'm down for you so ride with me,*
> *My enemies, your enemies*
> *Cause you ain't never had a friend like me"*

Bruno, one of Big Chucky's workout partners, caught up with him on the track and got his attention. Chucky pulled out one of his ear speakers that was blasting.

"Yo! Chucky they calling your name on the speaker saying, 'Roll it up,' and report to R&D."

Chucky didn't know what to expect, but he felt that he had won his appeal. He and Bruno reported to his unit and the C.O. Ms. Brown, told him that he had won his appeal and was being released. Chucky gave all of his commissary, the I-Pod and a couple pairs of tennis shoes to Bruno. He took a quick shower and got dressed in his brand-new Air Forces and a sweat suit. He put his paperwork, the only property he was leaving with, into a bag. Bruno walked with him to R&D. While sitting there waiting to be processed out he thought, *Now I can put my plan down, and make Barbara my woman.*

"Would you like to call someone before we take you to the Greyhound station?"

Chucky called Tammy, his Lil Mama, and told her to be at the Los Angeles Greyhound station by 3:45 P.M. and not to be late.

$

"OMG! Chucky, for you, I will be there early! I will be driving the green Magnum." she said.

He bought her that car while he was in prison. The plate read 'Mrs. Chucky'. Two Correction Officer's drove Chucky to the Greyhound bus station and gave him his bus ticket. He had fifteen minutes until his bus left. The Big K that was across the street was just what he needed because he needed some music to listen to. Big Chucky walked into the store, glad to be free. He watched ass and titties move throughout the place. He walked to the electronics department and bought a CD Walkman and Tupac and C-Bo's CD's. Then he left.

Once he sat down on the bus he looked at the view on the highway and played his favorite song 'You Ain't Never Had A Friend Like Me', and went into deep thought about how he would kill Pelle, Mista, Rocc, and all the other Luxury Boyz. When D-Money went to see him in the Phoenix, Arizona's federal prison. He said, "You ain't never had a friend like me."

D-Money told him that he would take care of the Luxury Boy's for killing Lamont, and Chucky's lil brother, Baby Chucky. He wondered why D-Money hadn't been back to see him since he said that he lived in Arizona. Chucky thought to himself. *Maybe shit got hot and he went to Brazil after all.*

Chucky's thoughts were interrupted by the Greyhound driver calling out the arrival of the Los Angeles station. Chucky got off the bus and walked through the station and out the front entrance. He took in all the movement and the downtown Los Angeles atmosphere. People were coming and going with their bags and luggage. Bums were begging for dollars and quarters. He thought to himself, *"Yup! Ain't nothing changed in the three and a half years I've been gone."* He quickly scanned the parking lot looking for the green Magnum. It was parked against the wall. The windows were so dark you couldn't see if anyone was in the car. He walked over to the car saying to himself, *'I know she see me.'* To his surprise she wasn't in the car. *'Damn, where is she?'* Just as he started to go inside and look for her, Tammy came from across the street with Chinese food that she got for him. She knew that was his favorite. As she walked up, she pressed the alarm button and unlocked the doors.

"Damn, Chucky, you got bigger. You look good baby!"

"I been big and I always have looked good!"

They both laughed.

"I see you still cocky as ever," she said, as they reached out to hug and kiss each other.

"Here, take the keys. You drive while I feed you. I know you ain't had no shrimp fried rice. You miss me? You miss this?" Tammy said as she pulled her skirt up showing her freshly trimmed pussy.

She fed Chucky untill he was full.

"So, you didn't miss me, huh? I know you missed this."

Tammy reached over and tugged at his sweats and pulled out his dick. She quickly lost it in her throat. Doing what she was best at; deep throating a dick. That's why Chucky kept her around.

"Uh aw!" Chuck squealed. "Yeah! I missed you and this bomb ass head you give. Yeah, suck Chuck's dick!"

Tammy swallowed the heavy thick fluid that Chucky shot out of his rod. He pushed her head down so that she couldn't come up for air and made her gag. When she finally came up for air, Tammy said, "Yeah, I know you miss this bomb ass head Nigga!"

Chucky drove to "The Alley" where they sold all types of clothes. Tammy bought Chucky every designer jean that she wanted to see his nice trimmed body in. She even bought some lace thong panties and bra sets. On the way to her house she played with herself while calling out Chucky's name.

"Ooh Chucky!" she screamed, as she grabbed at his man hood. Chucky was turned on. He pulled up at the store and bought his favorite drink, gin and juice, then speed off to Tammy's house. As soon as they got there Tammy made Chucky and herself a drink and then showered. She got out of the shower and walked in the bedroom with water dripping from her cocoa brown skin. As she dried off her body Chucky got a hard on. She put on her thong and bra set as Chucky sat on the bed sipping his gin straight and listened to Tupac's 'Thug Passion'. Tammy smiled bent over and grabbed her blunt from under the bed and lit it up. Chucky didn't smoke; he only drank.

"Let me hit that shit one time!"

"You don't smoke! I don't want you getting paranoid on this pussy," she said.

She got up, turned around, and bent over showing the back of her trimmed pussy. She walked up to Chucky and passed him the blunt. She laid down next to him, slide off her thongs, and fingered herself. Chucky blew smoke on her pussy and passed her back the blunt. Tammy sat on Chucky's dick that was standing straight up demanding attention. Chucky fucked Tammy harder and harder as he pulled her hair.

"You feel daddy's dick bitch?"

"Yea! Yea!" Tammy screamed.

He sexed every hole she had to offer: pussy, mouth, and ass. When Chucky was done, Tammy fell into a deep sleep. Chucky showered, put on his jeans outfit, told Tammy he needed to use her car and was out.

Chucky put in his Tupac CD into the car's CD player and played his favorite song, "You Ain't Never Had a Friend

Like Me" as he rolled to his baby mama's house. Once on her street he saw his oldest son, Charles Jr., playing football. He put him in the car and then asked. "Where yo brother, Charles?"

"He in the house pla'ing those games. That's all he do! He don't pla sports, he just pla those video games everyday after school."

Chucky handed him a $100 bill after asking about Jr's. grades and getting a good answer. They went into the house to see his other son and his baby mama. After playing a game with his second son, he handed him $100 as well. Then he went to see Rythim, his kids mom, but stopped to get twenty G's out of the fifty from his floor safe he had stashed in his sons clothes closet.

"Hey! Ree Boo!"

"What the! Why you didn't tell me you was getting out?"

"Because, I wanted to surprise you and pop up to see if you had some sucker up in my house."

"I see that jail made you lose your mind. So, I ain't gonna even reply to your nonsense," Rhytim said to big Chucky as she walked up on him, grabbed his waist, and planted kisses on his lips. The peck changed to a French kiss which lead to Chucky picking Rythim up and laying her down on the bed. He laid on top of her, then pulled her shirt off and her shorts down. He made love to the woman he would always love. The woman who would always have his back. Rythim never complained about him marrying her or him cheating, cause that's what niggas like Chucky do. But she knew when it came to her, she got what she wanted and needed, no matter what. Chucky jumped back in the shower and threw on some fresh new clothes.

He drove over to D-Money's baby momma's house to see where Money was hiding. Knock knock, was the sound made when Chucky's big knuckles hit the door. Trina answered the door.

"Chucky, you out!"

"Yeah, I won my appeal. Where's D-Money?"

"Come in," Trina said.

They sat in the kitchen. Trina offered him a soda or something to drink.

"Yeah, some gin." Chucky said.

"Sorry no gin. I don't drink."

"That's cool. You haven't heard from D-Money at all? Something's wrong with that."

"Yeah, I know the last time I seen him he gave me $40,000 and said I wouldn't see him for a while. Then he called a month later and said he lived in Arizona. That was ten months ago. But the thing that's strange is that Stacy been missing for that long too. Nobody has seen her neither. So, I don't know if they are together or they both dead or what?" she said, while almost crying with watery eyes.

"That's crazy," Chucky said, as he got up to leave.

Before he left he handed Trina five grand and told her that if she needed anything to call him on the number that he gave her with the money.

"We will be fine. It's been two years since he been gone. The insurance company is going to pay the $1,000,000 policy in two months. That will be three years," Trina said.

Chucky turned and left. He hit the square first for his gin and juice, then headed to Big Capone's house to let him know Chucky the Massacre is out and everybody in the Luxury hood has gots to die!

Chapter 11

Big Chucky went to the block of his old stomping grounds and he noticed that everything was different. The street had a luxurious look. All of the houses had been remodeled and painted. Once he was in front of Big Capone's girlfriend Queesha's house, Chucky poured himself a cup of gin and juice. Then he got out of the car and knocked on the door.

"Capone! ... Stop and see who's at the door!" Queesha said.

Capone pulled her shirt back over her big breast that he was sucking on while playing in her panties.

"Fuck! It better not be Eddie's smoked out ass beating on the door. Fucking up my groove.

Capone looked through the peep hole in the door and couldn't believe his eyes. 'What the fuck,' he thought, then he quickly opened the door.

"Big Chucky, when you get out? My nigga. Why you didn't tell me? I would have had a party lined up for you."

They brotherly hugged and both laughed.

"I don't want everybody to know I'm out. Come take a ride with me and have a drink. We need to talk."

Capone went to his bedroom that he shared with Queesha in her grandmother's home.

"Baby, Big Chucky just got out. I'm fist to roll out with him. We will finish what we started later."

Queesha frowned at the sound of Big Chucky's name.

"Always chasing behind them niggas! Bye!"

Capone turned around and said, "I'll be back."

Big Chucky and Capone sat in front of the house and talked about what the word was on the streets.

Capone told Chucky, "Word around here is that after Pelle was shot up and Jay Loc was killed, the L-Boyz killed Stacy and buried her on their ranch. Rock, Lil Q-Baller and Young Money are in jail. Q-Baller got killed when the Feds hit, and that bitch Tiff Tiff is supposed to be cooperating against them. You know Pelle's sister Pammy? She's a fed and she is the reason they hit the hood after her brother got shot."

"Damn! I knew it! I knew it! That bitch! Yeah Capone, we fixin' to get this money again around here. Let's go to the square and get some more gin and juice." Big Chucky said.

As they rolled to the store, Capone continued.

"Tiff Tiff told Goisha, Queesha's cousin, that Bloc, Young Money, and Mista killed and buried D-Money on their ranch too."

That shit had Chucky hot as fish grease. After leaving the store, he dranked the gin straight out the bottle.

"Yeah Capone … you say you and Queesha bout to have y'all a baby, huh? Well y'all gone need a car and y'all own place. You ready to run the city and kill anybody standing in your way?"

"Hell yeah, Big Chuck! You already know. Just tell me what need to be done and it's done."

As they rolled on the freeway, Chucky told Capone that he wanted Pelle, B-Locc, and every Luxury Boyz dead, but Mista was his personally. Rich Boy, aka Ricky, who used to work for D-Money and Big Chucky, now delivered for Pelle. Chucky told Capone he wanted Ricky immediately, and to gather up all the young homies, and open up shop out of the Greenhouse. That was the same house that Chucky was in front of when he went to jail. The house belonged to him, but was owned by the Jackie Company.

Chucky pulled up in front of Jackie's house and dialed her number. She never thought that he was out of jail or gave thought to the new number he called from, cause he was always getting new cell phones in jail.

"Hello Jackie. What you doing?"

"Oh, nothing just got out the tub and now I'm doing my toenails; rainbow colors. How are you doing? Do you need anything? You want me to send you more money?"

"Naw, in fact I'm sitting in front of your house."

"What! Stop lying. Why didn't you knock on the door then? How did you get out? You won your appeal?"

"Yeah, I won the appeal. I got out at 6 o'clock this morning. I didn't knock, cause I don't want your man getting mad at you," Chucky said, letting out a little chuckle. He knew that Jackie liked women."

"Yeah, right. I'm on my way downstairs."

Jackie went down with no bra on. She was wearing only lace thongs and a silk see through robe. She opened the door and walked out in the drive way. She could smell the kush blunt that Capone was smoking from the passenger seat.

"Damn, that's you Big Chucky?" Big Chucky got out of the car and gave Jackie a long hug. "Wow, you got bigger. Come in," Jackie said.

As she turned to walk back inside. Chucky told Capone he'll be right out in a minute.

"Don't trip my nigga. I got all night when it's about money."

Chucky had told Capone that he was going to give him $20,000, ten for himself and ten to spread in the hood. Big Chucky walked to the door which was halfway opened. Inside, Jackie had poured herself some vodka and cranberry juice and poured Chucky his favorite gin and juice. She sat Indian style next to him on the couch. Which gave view of her perfect Brazilian bikini wax with one pussy lip fully exposed.

"Why didn't you call and let me know you were out earlier."

"I wanted to surprise you."

"Well, you sure did that. I'm so glad you are out. How do you feel, Baby," she said and laughed. Then she got up and walked up stairs to her bedroom.

"Where's the Vette at?" he asked, loud enough for her to hear him upstairs.

"It's in the single garage on the other side. Come up stairs!" she screamed.

"I need about forty-five thousand. Do you have that much here?" He said, when he was at the top of the stairs. He fell silent when he seen Jackie lying on the bed in doggy position using her vibrator on her clit.

"Come here, Big Chuck. I'll get the money for you," she said, moaning.

Chucky swallowed the last of his gin and juice, then stripped butt naked, and laid under her waxed pussy and replaced the vibrator with his tongue.

"Ooh," she moaned, and quickly got in the sixty-nine position. Chucky, always wanted to fuck Jackie, but he didn't want to ruin their friendship. He took his time sexing her. He fucked her walking up and down the stairs, on the couch, on the floor, then back upstairs to the bed. Where he let out the biggest nut of his life.

"Wo-o-o-o," he howled, like a werewolf.

He laid next to Jackie for about five minutes.

"Get the keys to the Vette and the money. I forgot I had my homie sitting outside waiting. Let me take a shower. Do you still have some of my clothes in your closet?"

"Yeah, they are still in there with the cleaners plastic on them. I'll tell your friend to come inside while you shower. Damn, you got my coochie hurting," she said, laughing.

When Big Chucky went down stairs, Jackie was on the computer with a briefcase sitting on the desk next to her. She was wearing sweat pants and a t-shirt.

"Your clothes still fit. Huh?"

"Yeah, you know I was this size when I left the street. I'm just toned now."

"Your friend is in the kitchen eating Korean food. Yours is in the microwave."

Big Chucky never saw this side of Jackie before. They talked a lot during his almost three year bit. Sometimes they talked all-night. She fell in love with Chucky, but he didn't know it. She had planned on giving herself to him when he came home. Chucky walked up behind Jackie as she sat at her computer desk and kissed her lips and neck. Then he walked into the kitchen where Capone was placing his bowl in the dishwasher.

"I didn't mean to have you waiting that long, Pone."

"Don't trip Chucky. I was chilling, smoking, drinking and talking to Queesha about us getting us a house. Something like this house around the way. I was getting her prepared to move out and away from her granny."

"You ready to roll Pone?"

"Whenever you're ready."

"Let's roll."

Chucky grabbed the briefcase and the garage remote.

"That food was good Jackie. You made that?"

"Yep."

"I got to make some moves. I'll be gone for a couple of days. I'll call you tomorrow ... later." Chucky spit and was out the door.

Jackie sat there sprung and mesmerized by Chucky sexing her.

"Follow me, Pone. Here, take these keys and here go ten G's. I'mma give you ten more when I drop you off."

Chucky hit the remote, and the alarm to the Vette. Chirp chirp, was the sound the system made when he disarmed and unlocked the car. He jumped in. The car started like it did when he left in 2008. Jackie had it waxed and detailed every month like Chucky asked her to do. She also took it for tune up's and oil changes regularly. The appointment stickers were still on the windshield. Chucky backed out of the garage onto the other side of the two-car garage where Capone sat in the driver seat of the Magnum.

"Follow me!" Chucky yelled.

Then he smashed the Vette down the street. The money green paint shined like a mirror in the midnight. The shine bounced off the street lights. Big Chucky parked on the grass in front of Tammy's house and told Capone to park his car in front of the garage and to get in the Vette.

Chucky used the key on the key ring to open the front door. Then he took the key off the ring and put it in his pocket. He walked into Tammy's bedroom. She was asleep, lying on her stomach with the cover up to her knees. She was wearing some Ralph Lauren sports panties and bra. She looked sexy and Chucky wanted to wake her up with some dick in her, but instead he crept out the door to drop off Capone.

As they rode, they drank the last of the bottle of gin.

"Listen Capone. Make show you smoke Rich-Boy in front of everybody. He's around to let them know that the Greenland is on the green light. Alright? Ain't nobody gone say shit unless they want it too, and put the young homies to work. Let me know right now if you can handle this or if you gone bitch out."

"Come on Big Chucky. I'm with the business still, homie. I just been laying low since y'all been gone. But don't trip Capone. The slayer gone handle everything and we gone get the green paper in this hood. "

Big Chucky spit as he pulled up in front of Queesha's house.

"Hand me that briefcase on the back seat Pone, so I can give you the ten G's to spread to the young homies. Give twenty-five hundred to the shooters and one thousand to the slangers. I got to go out of town tonight to handle some business, but I'mma hit you in three days to see where we at ... alright? I'll let you know where to pick up the works. Alright homie ... I'm gone."

Chucky pulled off, bumping Jeezy's 'Go Getta' and thinking about fucking Tammy, how he was going to make Barbara Mayford the Correction Officer his wife, and how he was going to make his plan work. He dialed Barbara's number. It was 11:17 P.M. She answered after three rings.

"Hello."

"Hey baby. I didn't mean to wake you."

"Oh, it's okay,"

"Guess what!"

"What is it?"

"I'm out Ms. Mayford. I'm free!"

"What! How? You won the appeal?" she asked, laughing.

"Yeah, I knew I would."

"When did they let you go?"

"At six this morning. I was going to call you then, but I wanted to get myself together first. You know ... see my kids ... go get my wheels ... get me some clothes and a little spending cash. I'm ready to head your way, unless you was leading me along all this time."

"You know me better than that Charlie. Do you have a pen and a paper for my address?"

"Yeah," he said, while sitting in Tammy's driveway.

"Where or what city are you in, so I know what freeway you should take to get here, cause I stay in New Mexico."

"I'm in Compton, California but I know how to get to New Mexico. I'll call you when I'm in New Mexico. I'mma leave at four or five in the morning."

"Ok, see you soon ... bye."

Big Chucky got out and went inside the house and packed his bag with money and clothes. He laid his Coogi sweater and Coogi pants out so he could get dressed after he ran up in Tammy and got some rest. Chucky took off all his clothes. Tammy laid there snoring, now fully covered with the grey goose cover over her breast to her neck. Chucky stood over her with his dick in his hand, thinking about the night before when he was still in his jail cell. He thought how he had wished for some pussy. Now he stood next to some. That alone made his dick harder than a frozen neck bone. He stroked himself while looking at Tammy snoring. Then he pulled the cover all the way off of her. She never stopped snoring. She just turned on her side giving him better access and room to lay next to her. He laid next to her and rubbed on her ass, thigh, and stomach. Then he slid her panties down pass her thighs. Tammy was still snoring as he played with her pussy from behind. He rubbed his hard dick against her pussy and ass crack. He pulled her right thigh up a little for easy access to her pussy and shoved his log deep inside her. Tammy woke up taking a deep breathe. Then she cried out.

"What are you doing?"

Big Chucky just grabbed her by her neck and choked her.

"Shut up bitch! Take this dick!" he said, as he pumped and twisted her, making the pussy super wet.

He smothered Tammy with passionate kisses and bites till she exploded cum all over his dick. Then he quickly went from her pussy hole to her asshole. He rubbed the pussy juice (Tammy cream) with his hand and rubbed it in the exit zone. Like a werewolf when the moon comes out,

Chucky howled and grunted then he nutted in Tammy's asshole.

"You ain't ever had it like that," he said, out of breath gaining back his composure.

Tammy laid there and cried tears of pleasure and pain and then fell back to sleep. Chucky woke up three hours later. He got up, showered, and got dressed. He put $3,000 on Tammy,s nightstand then woke her up to say he had to go out of town.

"Fuck me again first before you go Chucky, please? How long you gone to be gone?"

"A week. I can't fuck you right now. I'm already late for traffic."

"Well, let me suck your dick," she said sitting up and unzipping Chucky's pants.

"Your pussy should be sore from the ass wiping I gave it last night."

"It is. That's why I want some more," she said, before deep throating Chucky's dick until it went from soft to rock hard. She did her magical work on him as she played with her clit. She made herself come at the same time Chucky came down her throat.

"Thank you, baby. Now you can go. Call me okay?"

Chucky washed his dick off and was gone.

Chapter 12

Detective Sturms set the recorder on the desk as Tiff Tiff bit her nails.

"State your name."

"Tiffany LaNette Baker, I went to school with Mista, Pelle, Rock, and B-Locc. They always been called Luxury Boyz. Mista, Pelle, and Rock posed to have killed D-Money's brother, L-Money, when we were in junior high. That started the Greenland and the Luxury Boyz to beefing. D-Money was locked up when it happened, so when he got out, the word is he had Pelle-Pelle shot up and J-Locc killed. That's why Mista, B-Locc, and Young Money killed D-Money.

"I went to Arizona with Young Money, following D-Money. I slept with D-Money and set him up. They had a car waiting for me and $10,000 in it for me setting up D-Money. They told me to go to their house in Vegas where I was arrested. Young Money said they was gonna bury D-Money on their ranch where Stacy is buried. That's all I know."

Detective Sturms stopped the recorder.

"You made the right decision Ms. Baker. You will be set up at a protection of custody witness house in Oklahoma. The gun charges against you will be dropped. Once you testify against the Luxury Boyz, you'll be given a new identity to start over with and of course $10,000."

$

Two Years Passed.

Tiff Tiff had been in four different states and over twenty different cities throughout each state. Mista was stuck up and robbed during a delivery in Detroit. He later found out that it was some kid out in the projects that robbed him. So he hired Stic Um-Up, a young stick man that turned hit man, who was referred to him by his business partner. Mista paid Stic Um-Up $50,000 to locate Tiff Tiff in any state or city and to terminate her rat ass. He gave Stic Um-Up Tiff's real name, nick name, and a picture of her and told him not to contact him until the job was done.

Stic Um-Up found her in San Antonio, Texas a year ago and watched her and the police's movement for three months before he made a move. The police hid her in a ranch house miles out of the inner city. There were four female officers on duty 24/7 protecting her. Tiff-Tiff was frustrated all the time not having any dick around. She was tired of fucking herself and playing with her clit. Every Wednesday at noon she would go to the stable, that was a half mile from the house near the grapevine that was grown on the farm, . Tiff rode the quad bike to the stable to get Big Fred. That's what she named the horse. After saddling up Big Fred, she would stroke the horses dick until it hung low. She couldn't believe how big a horse dick was. Her pussy would instantly jump and get soaking wet. She wanted badly to get under Big Fred somehow and slide that big dick inside her, but she was scared, so she played with herself until she came calling Big Fred's name.

One Wednesday Stic Um-Up crept up slowly and made his way inside the stable. What he saw when he went inside freaked him out. *'Dame this bitch is sick.'* he thought, *'Or horny as fuck.'* He walked up on Tiff-Tiff with his gun in hand.

"Hello, Tiff-Tiff."

She looked up eyes bucked and embarrassed.

"No! Don't move. Keep playing with yourself you freaky bitch. Man ... bitches are really horny hoes. You ain't had no dick since you fucked that officer and they put them female officers on duty, huh? You been fucking this horse?" He asked laughing. "What you call him, Big Fred? You a crazy bitch for real. But I'm gone let you get some of this dick though cuz. You turning me on, with that bald pussy you got. I know Fred don't mind. Do you Fred?

Stic Um-Up dropped his zipper and pulled out his dick and wiggled it.

"You want some human dick Tiff-Tiff? While you sucking it, I'll give you the message I have for you. Now sit up and say 'aw'."

Tiff-Tiff sat up staring down the barrel of Stic Um-Up's 44 Magnum. She put her mouth around Sticks dick and gagged when Stic tried to shove all his meat down her throat.

"I got a message from Mista. He says that you're a rodent and you must be terminated."

Tiff-Tiff was working that dick head and massaging his balls when she deep throated it and bit down as hard as her jaws could. She squeezed Stic's balls and tried to crack them. Stic was shocked and paralyzed for a moment with a piece of his dick on the ground. She got up, ran, and jumped on the quad and smashed off to the house. Stic came to and made his getaway thinking *This shit just went from business to personal now.*

$

That was a year and ten months ago. Now Stic Um-Up had found his prey again. He watched Tiff Tiff's daily moves for three weeks. The Feds had taken over Detective Sturms' case and then dropped it six months later. The government relocated Tiff Tiff to a suburban area in Detroit and gave her a new name, home, and social security number. But Tiff Tiff stayed in touch with her aunt and her mother.

Stic kidnapped and raped Tiff-Tiff's mom. He had her for eleven days when Tiff-Tiff finally called her mom to wish her a happy birthday. Stic put the phone on the speaker and held the phone to Tiff's mom's mouth with one hand and with his other hand held a rope around her neck. Stic whispered in her ear.

"Ask her what city is she in now and when can you see her, cause you need to sit down and talk to her about your illness."

"What illness momma? What's wrong? And I already told you I'm in Detroit. You can come to my house. You need to meet David and see your grandson anyway. Write down the address and get a plane ticket and come on down. You got a pen?"

"Yeah, I have one."

"It's 12824 Chester Avenue When you get to Michigan, just call and we gonna pick you up. We'll talk when you get here this weekend. Love you Momma."

"Love you too," Mrs. Baker said in tears.

Stic Um-Up hung up the phone and smiled. He thought, *She in my hometown, that's good news.*

"Now that wasn't so bad, was it Momma? You ready for your fix. I see you scratching and fidgety."

He filled the syringe with heroin, but not with the cut that he had been giving her. This cut was raw footage that would cause her to over dose. Stic made it look as if she had been getting high again and was raped by another addict. He put the syringe to her neck and squeezed the rope. He made her veins pop out and then he pushed the dope into her neck. Her eyes rolled to the back of her head. She fell backwards onto the bed unconscious. Nothing was covering her pussy except the bottom of her shirt that was thigh high. Stic Um-Up rapped Norma for an hour with his patched together dick; that almost had no feeling. After he was satisfied, he showered and left the room. He left Norma lifeless on the bed in the run down druggy motel then headed to his hometown, Detroit.

Chapter 13

Tiffany Baker, aka Tiff-Tiff, was given the new name Sandra Williams. Every morning she walked her son, Demetrius, to school and then went on a jog through the park and around the dirt lots of the up and coming housing development. Stic Um-Up sat in his old pickup truck waiting to put his plan in motion. He knew that Tiff would be running through the development in 10 minutes. He had watched and timed her for three weeks. He set his timer and got out of the truck in a construction outfit. He dialed seven digits.

"What's *Luxury*?"

"What up Mista? This Stic. Look business is closed by noon, so that other check should be ready for me by tomorrow when I'm in town."

"Damn Stic, it's been three years. But if the business is sold then you'll get paid. I'll have my folks come out to you by Friday, that's two days. Is that cool?"

"Yeah, Strait."

"Alright … I'll hit you tonight and let you know who's coming and where to meet him."

Stic put his phone in the truck and got into position. He had two minutes till Tiff would jog by. Three minutes later, one minute off of Stic's time, Tiff hit the corner jogging. It was 7:47 a.m. and nobody else was out. As soon as Tiff got about five feet away, Stic flagged Tiff down with his construction hat on.

"Excuse me madam you can't run through this area. It's dangerous around here!"

"Oh … ok. I stay across there. That's why I run through here. It's my short cut …."

Before Tiff could get the word home out her mouth, Stic tazed her. Tiff dropped straight to the dirt. Stic tazed her again and knocked her out. When Tiff-Tiff woke up she was asshole naked and had a headache. She was lying on her back and tied up to a slab of wood. All she remembered was walking her son to school and jogging home. Stic broke her thought of trying to remember what had happened, when he entered the room with his tool box, chain saw, and trash bags, and a big smile on his face.

"What's up Sandra, Tiffany, or is it Tiff-Tiff? You remember me?"

Tiff tried to say please don't kill me, but couldn't cause of the ball straped in her mouth. She just started pouring out crocodile tears. She knew she would never see her son, Demetrius, or her husband, David, again. She always told herself that life was too good to be true.

"Stop that crying Tiff and go out like the gangster bitch you is or was. Your momma took hers like a big girl."

Tiff cried even harder now knowing that she got her momma killed.

"Look Sandra, I'm gone keep it real with you. I'm not gonna torture you or beat you. But I am going to give you your last pleasure. I'm going to fuck you with this dick that feels nothing for at least an hour. Then I'm going to fuck you with the Magnum, cause I know how you like freaky shit. Next I'm going to blow your brains out of your head. It was strictly business until you bit off my dick. Now it's personal bitch, even though that's against my rules ... but what the hell. I'll break um for you. You ready to get this party started? I was against this, but you a rat rotten bitch. Here's a message from the Luxury Boyz. They said, 'Drink piss, bitch'," Stic said smiling while he pissed on Tiff's face.

After emptying his bladder on Tiff, he squeezed baby oil all over her naked body. Then he untied her legs. He told her that if she kicked him he was going to torcher her by taking one eye out of its socket and then make her eat her own eye as he burned off her nipples. Tiff didn't move. She knew that he meant business. Stic Um-Up took the wrench he had in his hand and put baby oil on it and stuck it in Tiff's ass. At first he moved it very slowly and then at a faster motion. Tiff cried out from the pain and from the pleasure. It turned her on. Once the anal was fully open, he pushed the wrench up Tiff's pussy causing her to let out an, "Aaaww!", through the mouth ball strap. Then Stic raped Tiff for two hours until he was about to nut. He then pulled out and ejaculated in both of her eyes. Stic then stuck in his 44 Magnum and fucked her with it till she passed out. He woke her up after about ten minutes and then blew her brains out. He then cut her up with the chainsaw, bagged her body parts and cleaned up the blood. He buried her body under the drive way that was ready to be covered in concrete. Then he left dialing seven digits.

"What's luxury?"

"This Stic Um, that business is handled. Where should I meet your boy?"

"He gone be in the projects Wednesday on the Westside in Building D, Apartment 337. His name Kev-Loc. I'm gone Stic … be cool."

Mista had already told himself that Stic had to go. He was a loose end. After hearing what happened to Norma, Tiff's mom, just made it even easier. He told Stic Um-Up to leave Tiff's moms out of it. After Tiff bit his dick it became personal to Stic and he broke all the rules for revenge. Mista, hit seven digits and called Kev-Loc. Kev-Loc was one of the younger Luxury Boyz on the block for Mista.

"What's luxury?"

"Look Kev. I need you to make a move for me. I need you to come up to the dealership to pick up a car. I'll give you the business in person when you get here. Come right now, seven."

Kev-Loc and Brown Rag pulled up 30 minutes later. They walked inside the dealership, to the front desk where Sharie, a Honduran Latino and Black dime piece, sat.

"What's luxury?" Brown Rag said.

"Where Mista?" Kev-Loc said.

Sharie spoke to Mista on the intercom and told him that Kev was there to see him.

"Send him in."

Kev-Loc walked to the back office. Brown Rag stayed up front and tried to spit some game on Sharie. When Kev-Loc walked in the office, Mista was sitting on the edge of his desk talking to Ebony.

"I'll call you later babe. Ok, Love!"

Mista embraced Kev with a brotherly hug and the Luxury Boy hand shake then walked around his desk and sat in his plush executive chair. Kev sat in the other plush chair on the opposite side of the desk.

"This is what I need you to do Kev, go to Detroit to the address that's in that briefcase right there. There's fifty G's in there. That's for you. You gone pay the fifty to a dude name Stic Um-Up, but don't let him leave with the money. Put an end to him. Keep the fifty as payment. Can you handle that?"

"Don't trip Mista. I got you. It's done."

"Good. Make the move in that grey Buick Lacrosse, and that's yours to keep. I need you there in two days. Call on the business line when you handled that. Marcus is there waiting for you. There's ten G's in the Buick for him in the trunk."

Mista walked Kev-Loc to the front.

"Brownie, leave Sharie alone. Nigga, she told me you ain't got enough color for her," Mista said, fucking with Brown Rag for being light skinned.

"That's my future wife. Ain't that right, Mommie?" Brownie said.

Sharie just smiled. Once all three of them were outside, Mista said, "Don't take Brownie. I need him in the city. Take you a female for the ride, alright Kev-Loc?"

"Yeah, that's what I was thinking too. Plus getting some head all the way there," Kev-Loc said. He laughed as he got in the Buick. Brown Rag got in a Lexus.

Kev-Loc hit the highway at 7 p.m. that night and he made it to Detroit in two days. Marcus had everything staged just how Mista told him he wanted it. Kev-Loc sat on the couch and smoked a spliff while giving directions to Stic Um-Up to get to the apartment where he was.

"You in the hallway?"

"Yeah."

"Alright come inside. The door is unlocked just lock the door behind you. I'm on the couch rolling me a spliff for my ride back."

Stic Um-Up put a bullet in the chamber of his 9 Berretta, then he put it at his waist for quick access. He opened the door cautiously he thought to himself, *I hope Mista and these fools ain't trying to dead me, cause I ain't going out easy.* Kev-Loc stood up when Stic opened the door.

"What's up? My man, Mista, sends his appreciation with his top lieutenant — me."

After giving each other a greeting, Kev asked Stic if he wanted to hit the spliff.

"I don't smoke or drink. You got to keep a level head in my line of work," Stic said.

He looked around and felt that something wasn't right.

"Let's get to business."

Kev-Loc pushed the briefcase toward Stic.

"It's fifty G's in there. Go ahead and count it if you want."

"Naw, that would be disrespectful. You didn't come all the way out her to short me."

Stic closed the case and said, "Tell Mista the number will always be the same."

As he attempted to walk to the door, Marcus came out the kitchen and busted four shots: two hit Stic in the back of his head and neck, and the other two hit him in the shoulder and spine. Stic was dead before he hit the floor. Kev and Marcus rolled up Stic Um-Up in the rug. Marcus laid the rug down before Kev-Loc got there like Mista had instructed him to do. Kev gave Marcus ten G's plus another five to get rid of the body by himself, then he headed back to the city. While on the highway driving back, Stephanie sucked Kev-Loc's dick. He hit seven digits.

"What's luxury?"

"On my way back. The business sold alright ... Seven!"

The call ended.

Chapter 14

Mista sat holding his son that Kelly gave birth to. His wife, Ebony, gave birth to a little girl. Now that he had a son, he stayed around his boy more than the girls, even though they were *"Daddy's girls"*. His first born to Raven, Magazine, was spoiled rotten. Emonie, his other daughter by Ebony, was only six months old and also spoiled. Mutasur Jr. was only one years old.

Mista's cellphone went off.

"Hello."

"You have a prepaid call from Money. You will not be charged for this call. If you wish to accept this call, press five. If you do not want to receive any more calls from this prisoner, press seven or press five to accept."

Mista pressed five.

"Money, What's luxury?"

"Shit, Mista, it's all bad. I don't mean to fuck your day up, but Rock gone. He dead, Mista."

"What! Money! What the fuck happened?"

"They say some fools caught Rock by himself coming from the visiting hall. Man ... they poked him twenty times. B-Locc, he in the hole for a year. I sent word to him. I'm ready to kill something, Mista. I don't give a fuck about them recording this conversation. That's my brother — my mother's son — gone. Mista, they say some DC niggas did it. Nobody betta cross me or get in my fucking way. I'm gonna get every detail. Bury my brother Mista and send some pictures. I'm gone."

"Hold up. Look just lay low for me. Keep yo head up. Much love!"

The call ended. Mista looked down at his son as he fell into a daze. He thought about the memories of his fallen Luxury Boyz. A tear crept down his cheek past the two-permanent tear drop tattoos on his left check. He put his son down and went into the restroom to wash his face. Then he picked up Lil Mista and took him to his little sister-in-law. He went to his private room to make himself a drink and to call Pelle. After telling Pelle he was coming to his house, he went upstairs to his bedroom where Kelly was watching television. Mista had the whole bottle of Remy in his hand and downed it. He drunk it down like it was orange juice. Kelly was not aware of the bad news. She cut off the TV and walked to Mista who was sitting on the couch and tried to give Mista some of her good. But Mista pushed her to the side.

"What! Raven already drained you? Fuck that bitch! I had your son!" Kelly said.

Mista was already pissed off. He hauled off and slapped the spit out of Kelly's mouth and then walked out the door. He got in the 650 and smashed out to Pelle Pelle's in Alabama. He almost lost control of the car he sped so fast out of the driveway. Mista was so pissy drunk, he didn't know how he got to Pelle's house. He beat on the door with the empty bottle of Remy. Pelle opened the door.

"Damn, my nigga how you drive here?"

"I drove," Mista slurred, as he staggered in. "I need to piss. Where the toilet at?"

"Down there. Use Pete's."

Mista went to the bathroom and pissed on everything outside of the toilet. Then he went out to talk to Pelle.

"Pelle, they took our boy."

Pelle walked to the "men's room"; that's what he called the room that no woman had ever entered. That's where he and Pete drank, talked, and did what men like to do. Uncle P went into the room with his "no throw-up drink": lemon, squirt, pickle juice and a shot of 7 Up with crushed ice.

"You'll never throw up when you drink this. You lucky Carla is still here cause you would be cleaning up all that piss on the floor in that restroom Blackman," Uncle P said, as he gave the drink to Mista.

Carla is the maid. Uncle P called all Black men "Blackman", cause he was once a Black Panther. Pelle and Mista wore the same size clothes and shoes, so Pelle gave Mista some brand new clothes to change into: Polo socks, draughs, pants, a belt, a shirt, and shoes. They both wore size seven shoes and size 33/34 pants. Mista showered in the mens restroom and got dressed, then went upstairs.

Pelle-Pelle was in the kitchen talking with Uncle P. Mista sat at the large table that was capable of sitting fourteen people. Carla put a plate of shrimp spaghetti in front of Mista.

"When you start eating shrimp spaghetti, Pelle?"

"I had Carla make it cause I know my brother loved it."

Mista looked at Pelle. They stared at each other without saying a word. They were speaking with their eyes. Pelle went up to his room where his wife was and kissed her neck and said. "See you in three days." She would fly down to attend the funeral and help Miss Fuller cook for the after burial.

Pelle, Uncle P, and Mista jumped in Pelle's Range Rover and smashed it to the city. As soon as they got to the city, they bought something to drink, then they went to Q-Ball's grave to pour some liquor on it. After that, they hit Miss Fullers house. Pelle-Pelle pulled on Luxury Street and parked in front of Miss Fuller's house. They all got out of the car and was walking toward the driveway when Brownie yelled out from across the street at Luxury Girl Tammy's house.

"What's luxury!?"

Then Brownie walked across the street to greet his homies. They all went inside. Miss Fuller hugged them and asked if anyone was hungry, just like she did every time they went to her house. Monique and Raven was in the kitchen cooking gumbo, fried chicken, peach cobbler, cakes and all types of food.

Uncle P, Pelle, and Brownie went to the backyard where some of Rock's cousins and aunties was. Betty is Rock's, mother's, sister. She moved to Texas. She used to be Uncle P's girlfriend back in the day. When Uncle P saw Betty, he went into his player mode. Pelle and Brownie sat down and talked with Rock's cousins, Angela and Christine, while they smoked spliffs and sipped on Coronas.

Mista stayed inside and talked with Miss Fuller. He told her that the funeral expenses was on him. Then he walked to the kitchen door and called Raven. They walked into the front room.

"How long you been here baby?"

"Since yesterday. When Monique called me crying, I came to help my friend and Miss Fuller get through this. Kelly will be here tomorrow."

Damn! Mista thought to himself. *This shit fixin' to hit the fan. I need to tell Raven.* But he didn't.

Later that night Mista and Raven went and got a room. Uncle P and Pelle stayed at Miss Fuller's house. Mista slept after sexing Raven. Raven stayed awake. She sat up against the headboard and starred at Mista while he slept. Then she got up and got two ice buckets full of melted ice and cold water, pulled the covers off Mista, and poured one of the buckets of water and ice all over him.

"What the fuck Bitch! Is you stupid?"

"I'll show you a bitch," she said.

Then she poured the other bucket in his face. "Who is Lil Mutasur and Emonie, Mista? You been taking my daughter to see some brother and sister she got?"

Mista just laid there quiet. Raven reloaded the ice bucket and poured another bucket on him.

"Look! Raven, I been wanting to tell you."

"Tell me what Mista? Yo nasty dick ass been fucking two different bitches bare and fucking me bare? You punk bitch … and then had two kids on the side! Then I had to find out by some gossiping bitches, that I'm 'pose to know who one of the bitches is. I don't need this shit Mista, or you! I own my own shit! That's my house in Atlanta! I'm through with you and your shit!" Raven screamed and shouted.

Raven slept on the couch in the penthouse suit. At 7 A.M. the next morning, Mista woke Raven up with his tongue between her legs. She wanted so bad to get up, but was already moaning and cuming. They showered got dressed and smashed it to Miss Fuller's house. Uncle P, Pelle, and Mista went to the dealership, parked the Rover, and jumped in a 500 to ride around town in. Then they went to the liquor bank and got every drink you could think of for the after burial party. After dropping off the beer and liquor at the hall where the party would be held, they headed to get fitted for their suits. Mr. Phae, the tailor, made perfect measurements for Mista, Pelle, and Uncle P. When Mr. Phae finished, it was 11 P.M.

Chapter 15

The Luxury Boyz went to the square where everyone hung out on Fridays. Mista pulled into the lot and parked by Brownie, Kev-Loc, and Lady Luxury. They all got out of the car, popped the trunk, and took out three bottles of Remy and four bottles of Cristal. They were talking and cracking jokes. Rich Boy was hollering at some hoes that were sitting in their car. He didn't see Capone walking towards him until they were two feet apart. Capone said. "This is my city and this a green light." When Rich Boy turned around Capone opened fire. He shot him twice in the head. Then he stood over him and shot Rich Boy five more times. Green Eyes pulled up and Capone jumped in the car. Before they turned out of the lot, Capone opened fired with the MAC-10. He aimed at Mista and the Luxury Boyz. Everybody had ducked down when they heard the first shots, so they couldn't see, who shot who, or who shot back, or even who got hit.

Penny ran over to Rich Boy crying and screaming, "Ricky, don't die! Get up!"

By the time Mista and everybody got to where Rich Boy laid, one of the girls sitting in the car said, "It was Capone ... one of the Greenlands."

She wanted the Luxury Boyz to get him cause he shot up her truck.

"He said that it's his city and 'It's a green light on all Luxury Boyz!'" she said, adding extra to what she heard. She did not know that she spoke Capone's words.

Kelly made it to town with Mista's son for the funeral. She stayed at her old house (that she still owned) in the city. Pelle was in town for the funeral too. Kimmy was at Miss Fuller's house, so Mista dropped Uncle P. and Pelle off at Miss Fuller's and smashed off to the house where his wife and daughter were. In his mind and heart he knew shit was gonna get crazy when it hit the fan, but he said, "Fuck it." He knew that Ebony knew about Kelly and Raven so he was straight on her end.

$

Capone sat on the edge of his bed smoking a spliff, while trying to call Big Chucky on his cell for the sixtieth time.

"Yeah, who diss?"

"This Capone. Why you ain't been answering your phone?"

"That boy ain't no moe, but word is that Mista is looking for me."

"Alright. Look get on the Greyhound and get a ticket to New Mexico. Call me when you there."

Chucky hung up. Big Chucky had been putting his work in for the last two weeks.

"That was my cousin. He and his girlfriend gonna come down here for the weekend to ride back with me, Babe. I can't wait for you to meet Cory with his comedian ass. For real he a straight clown."

Capone hit up Big Chucky when he was in New Mexico. Big Chucky went to pick up Capone in his off road truck while blasting his favorite song. Capone knew Chucky was there when he heard the music when he pulled up into the parking lot.

"Natalie that's gotta be my nigga. Come on."

He got off the bench, took off his hood and threw up both his hands so that Big Chucky could see him. Big Chucky pulled up to the curb. Capone opened the door and let Natalie in the back seat, the he jumped in front.

"Sup, Big Chuck? My nigga."

"Sup, Capone? Who that fine girl with you?"

"Who? That bitch? That's the home girl Nauty. She Jack's daughter."

"Black Jack?"

"Yeah. You know that nigga overdosed, so she and her mother moved in with Jack's mom in the Green. She good though and down for whatever. The head and the pussy is bomb. Yeah, though. I smoked that nigga Rich Boy at the square right in front of everybody. As I was leaving I seen Mista and Pelle, so I emptied the rest of the clip aiming at them. Now they riding through the hood hitting some of the homies, so I been laying low at Natalie's house every since, waiting to get in contact with you."

"Look … when we get to the house, you are my cousin and she is your wife … okay?"

"Ok."

"That's what I told Barbara already. She a police, Federal Correctional Officer, so ain't no spliff smoking when she's there ... only drinking and cigarettes."

Big Chucky pulled up at the store and told Pone to get some cigarettes, two twenty four packs of Corona, and some ranch dressing.

"Tell Cezar I said to give you that. He's the one behind the register. Sup, Natalie? So old Black Jack yo pops, huh? Yeah, that was a good man. He taught me how to get this paper when I was a teenager. But you look like you White."

"My mother is White and well you know my daddy's Black. I'm just high-yellow."

"Yeah, cause you do got some of his looks."

Capone came out with the groceries and got in the car.

"Man here. That shit look bomb too. Did he grow that?"

"Yeah, that's my weed connect. When we leave, this is the product we taking down to the land."

Barbara made fried fish, baked potatos, salad, and shrimp and everyone ate until they were stuffed. Capone and Nauty went outside to smoke their spliff and cigarettes. Barbara had to be at work at six in the morning. She had to leave within thirty minutes in order to be at work on time. It took five hours to get there, but she wanted to get some rest at her sister's house. That where she would stay till her quarter was up in thirty days. Big Chucky walked Barbara out to the car. She was driving the Vette. Barbara could smell the spliff, but didn't say anything about it. She knew Chucky smoked and she respected how he didn't smoke around her or in the house.

"Bye baby. I'll call while I'm driving."

"Ok, drive safe and don't speed. The police will pull you over in this car."

"Ok."

They kissed and Officer Mayford disappeared in the night. Big Chucky smiled and thought to himself how well his plan was coming together. Plus, fucking Nauty was all he could think about. Chuck walked to the side of the house where Capone and Nauty were standing and smoking. "Let's go in. Barbara's gone. We can smoke inside now," Big Chucky told Capone and Nauty. Chucky gave them a choice to share a guest room together or each take a separate room. "I'll take my own room," Nauty said. She chose an upstairs guest room down the hall from Barbara and Chucky's master bedroom.

Capone and Chucky sat downstairs in the den where Chucky put down the mission at hand. The plan was for Capone to go to the store tomorrow and get twenty bricks of cocaine and four hundred pounds of weed from Cezar. Nauty would drive the car back to the city while Capone and Big Chucky followed her.

Natalie went downstairs wearing some boxers and a sports bra. Big Chucky wanted to fuck, but held back right then. They drank and smoked spliffs till Capone fell out. Nauty was still at it.

"Let me go to sleep 'for I fall out too," Nauty said.

"I'm bout to jump in the shower. You want to get in?"

"Naw ... I would but I'm cool."

Nauty went to her room and laid down. Big Chucky jumped in the shower for about ten minutes. He got out soaking wet and walked into Nauty's guest room. She had fallen asleep and was out cold. Chucky pulled off her boxers exposing her pretty little pussy and stomach. Nauty didn't wake up, but she had a smile on her face as if she felt Chucky or knew what was going on. Chucky stroked his dick in her face until it was rock hard. He parted her lips with his dick head and she woke up stunned.

"You know you want this. I saw the way you be watching me. Open your mouth."

Nauty opened her mouth and Chucky plugged her throat. He put one hand behind her head and made her gage and choke. He kept on forcing himself down her throat. Then in one motion, he entered her pussy, grabbed her neck with both hands and chocked her while he pounded her insides. He pulled himself out, folded her up in a ball and went deep in her ass. She screamed and cried from both pleasure and pain. When Chucky pulled his dick out it was covered with blood. He walked out saying nothing and jumped back in the shower. Then crashed out.

Nauty got up and tried to pee. She was in so much pain from the beating Chucky put on her guts and butt. Getting in the shower made her feel so much better. As she thought about what just happened, it made her pussy wet.

Chapter 16

Hard Rock's funeral was so packed that some people couldn't even sit. So some stood in the back of the room and out front. Forty cars drove down Central to bury the fallen Luxury Boy. At the after burial, all three of Mista's baby momma's were there. Mista and some known rappers were taking pictures, with Rock's photo in the background of him sitting on the hood of his Q7. The commotion in the middle of the hall took everybody's attention. Mista saw it was Raven and Ebony arguing.

"I don't care if you had a baby by Mista! I had his first-born daughter and is his wife!"

"No, you got that wrong! I knew about you and Kelly, his son's mother! So I had a marriage data check to see if he was married to one of you before we got married! You can't see this seven carat ring on my finger? So, you the baby momma and **I'm the wife!**"

Before Raven could swing, Mista stood in between them. Miss Fuller pulled Raven aside and said, "It ain't the time or the place for this."

Mista took Ebony, his wife, to his mother's house and then left. Ebony carried her daughter inside with tears in her eyes.

"What have that boy done now?" Mrs. Gibbson asked.

Ebony told her everything. Mrs. Gibbson called Mista.

"You are a married man now. You chose your wife, so get back to her."

"I'll be there later. I got to handle some business," Mista said.

Mista pulled into Miss Fuller's driveway and got out of the car. When he went inside, Kelly and Raven where in the kitchen arguing. Miss Fuller and Monique was standing between them. When Mista left the after burial party earlier with Ebony, Raven started drinking Moet straight from the bottle. Then she walked over to Kelly and hit her over the head with the bottle.

"Bitch, you fucked Mista and had a baby by him. You been smiling in my face all day today and yesterday."

Raven was ready to leave, but Miss Fuller insisted that Raven talked it out with Kelly before leaving, so Raven stood there holding her purse. When Mista walked in the kitchen the calmness that Raven felt turned to rage and out of nowhere she pulled the Baby 45 pistol out of her purse which Mista bought her and taught her how to use. She aimed it at Mista and pulled the trigger three times. Fire shot out the barrel and all three bullets hit Mista in the chest. Uncle P, grabbed the gun from Raven and pushed her backwards. Raven stood there stunned with tears falling down her cheeks. She was in shock from what she had just done. Miss Fuller dropped to the ground and talked to Mista who was fading away.

"Call the ambulance!" Miss Fuller screamed.

Raven dropped to her knees next to Mista.

"I'm so sorry! I love you, Mista!" she cried.

"I love you too. I love all of y'all," said Mista. Those were his last words.

Pelle Pelle and Uncle P had to restrain Kelly from attacking Raven. The police and paramedics rushed inside.

"She shot him. She killed my son's father!" Kelly screamed.

Pelle felt the weight of the world was on his shoulders. He took a swig of the Remy straight out the bottle and lit a Newport. He dialed Miss Gibbson's number.

"Hello."

"Is Miss Gibbson there?"

"Yes she is. May I ask who's calling?" asked Ebony.

"Yes, this Pelle."

"Oh hey Pelle."

"Hey."

"Pelle, I know that boy Mista had you call here. You tell him his momma said, 'Come and attend to his family, his wife and daughter, cause they his family'. Where is he? Give him the phone,"

Pelle couldn't take it. He broke down saying, "He gone Miss Gibbson! Raven just shot and killed Mista."

Miss Gibbson dropped the phone and Ebony picked it up.

"Hello, who is this?"

"This Pelle, Ebony. Raven just shot and killed Mista at Miss Fuller's house."

"No!!" Ebony cried.

Pelle just hung up the phone and watched the police walk Raven out, who was crying hysterically.

$

Two days passed since Mista was killed. Pelle went out to his house to think. It seemed to him that, all the luxury in the world didn't mean anything. You can't take it with you. You can lose your soul chasing and trying to capture it. But he couldn't stop now. Luxury living was all he knew and he wasn't giving it up. Pelle showered and got fresher than fresh air. He had to be at the dealership because he was taking over operations of it that day.

Pelle and Uncle P walked out of the airport and jumped in the Chrysler Imperial that Deon, the dealership's transporter, was driving.

"Alright Oscar, I'll see you at the funeral tomorrow," Pelle said and ended the call.

He sat back in the soft leather luxury chair in his new office and looked at a blown up picture of Mista on the wall.

"I will never take your picture down my brother. Your memory and the legend we started will live forever."

He fought off the tears, closed his eyes, and took a deep breath. Just then the phone rang and shook him out of his thoughts.

"Hello!"

"You have a prepaid call from Money. You will not be charged for this call. This call is from a prisoner in a Federal prison. If you do not wish to receive any calls from this person, press seven. If you wish to accept, press five. Pelle pressed five, thinking, *Damn, all that before saying press five, to accept, damn.*

"Young Money. What's Luxury?"

"Nothing but the Luxury Boyz that's left," Young Money said. That hit Pelle *hard.*

"Yeah, I hear you Money. How you, Lil Q, and B-Locc holding up?"

"We just walking this time down, but niggas going crazy losing our brothers back to back," he said, while fighting off tears. "Look Pelle you all we got out there. So make sure you do whatever got to be done to survive man, cause I can't take another Luxury Boy falling."

"Yeah, I hear you. Look, y'all just walk that time down, so y'all can get back to living Luxury. I'm holding down the fort. Tell B-Locc and Lil Q, 'Mista going out in luxury. Like Rocc did in a rose platinum casket'. ... Seven."

The call ended. Shari buzzed his office phone to tell Pelle that Detective Sturms was there to see him. Sturms went to the dealership twice a month to harass Mista about what happened to Tiff and D-Money, but really had nothing. He was just trying to get Mista to incriminate himself.

"Send him in Sharie," Pelle said, while lighting his cigar and filling the office with smoke.

"Well, if it isn't the great Shapell Walters, aka Pelle. I see you've taken over the crime enterprise for the Luxury Boyz, huh?

"What crime enterprise? You're confusing our legitimate business with someone else's business. We just sell cars here, and clothes and shoes at our other businesses."

"Well, I know the Luxury Boyz started those businesses with drug money and the Luxury Boyz are responsible for the murders of Danny Ford, aka D-Money, and of a witness, Tiffany, aka Tiff-Tiff, an ex-Luxury Girl turned informant."

"Mr. Sturms, I respect you doing your job, but don't come to my business with all your assumptions. As you know, I'll be burying my best friend tomorrow. So leave your card on the desk. And if I can assist you with any information about your murdered victims, I will give you a call."

Detective Sturms put a card on the desk then turned around to leave. Before he opened the door he turned around and said.

"Mista is gone now and your other crime partners are in a federal prison. You know when I get you (and I will get you) you're going to get the rico and crime organizer, which will give you life — but if you can give me Oscar, you won't get life."

Then he walked out. Uncle P walked in after Detective Sturms left.

"What was that about? Is everything cool?"

"Yeah, that pig with black skin just doing his usual harassing. Let's roll. We 'pose to be at Mr. Phaes to get tailored. Call Kev and Brown, and have them meet us there."

Uncle P and Pelle jumped into the flying spur Bentley. Uncle P was behind the wheel. He smashed to Mr. Phae's tailor shop.

Chapter 17

Big Chucky, Capone, and Naughty drove to where the car packed with twenty G's, and sixty bricks of weed was parked in Albuquerque, New Mexico. It was a hour ride from where they were. Chucky watched the rearview mirror and thought about how he had Nauty screaming last night. He pulled into a gas station and told Capone to pay for the gas and gave him a $100 bill. Chucky pumped the gas while smoking a Camel. Capone walked up and said to him.

"Damn Chucky, you gone blow us all up. Let me pump the gas."

"You can drive too," Chucky said. "I'm about to get some bomb head from Nauty."

"I know you ain't got no feelings attached. Do you?"

"Naw. Come on homie, my wifey fist to have my first born."

"Good, cause I was gone mark your ass off if you said anything different"

Chucky jumped in the back seat with Nauty. Capone jumped in behind the wheel and hit the highway. Chucky fired up a spliff and passed it to Nauty. He played with her nipples and pulled out his dick. He held it in his hand, then grabbed the back of Nauty's neck and pushed her down to serve the dome. Within seconds she was gagging and begging for some air. But Chucky wasn't letting up till she drank everything he shot in her throat. Nauty fell asleep after Chucky got the pussy. Chucky jumped over to the front passenger seat.

"Right there Pone. Turn left. Pull in the back of that white house."

Later that night they hit the road. Nauty had four dogs in cages. A toy poodle, a boxer, a Chihuahua, and a pit bull to throw the police off by telling them she was a dog breeder and had just came from breeding down in Mexico. The ride went smooth. They dropped the car off and went to Natalie's house. As soon as Nauty's mom saw Capone, she wanted some Oxy. Pone gave her the pills, while Nauty and Chucky went into her bedroom.

"Hey Capone, is mom's gone trip with us hanging out here?"

"Naw, her ass be so gone on them Oxy. She don't know who be here. Let's roll to the hood for a minute. Nauty gone drive."

They hit the square and got some drank, Chucky's favorite, gin and juice. When Chucky and Nauty came out, Chucky saw Be-Be and Leonard.

"Come on, Nauty, let me say something to these mutha fuckers. What's up, Be-Be? What's up L-Dog?"

When they heard and saw Chucky, they both swallowed hard and spoke back.

"Whaaa, what's up Big Chucky? You out?" L-Dog said.

"What's up Chucky?" Be-Be, said unpleasantly.

Be-Be hated Big Chucky every since the night she and her friend went to the beach with Capone and Chucky. Capone and Lisa was already a couple, so they laid a blanket on the beach and got busy. But Be-Be and Chucky were just starting to talk. They sat in the car smoking and drinking till Chucky thought he deserved some pussy. He started touching Be-Be on her leg and neck. She stopped him before he thought he was gonna get some. Next thing she knew, he had a gun to her head and made her suck his dick and swallow all his cum. Then he raped her. She never told anyone and hated him ever since.

"Yeah, Chucky the Massacre is back. I heard you working for Mista ... the Luxury boy? And don't lie nigga or say the wrong thing, cause I'm gone knock your mark ass out right in front of your bitch, then, I'll wake you up so you can watch me fuck her again."

That hit L-Dog hard. Be-Be never mentioned fucking Big Chucky. He wanted to pull his three eighty bad, but didn't want to catch that right hook trying to pull.

"Yeah, I used to work for Mista, the Luxury Boy, but Mista is dead now. His baby momma, Raven, shot and killed him four days ago. So I don't work for the Luxury Boyz no more."

"Who told you? Shit, everybody know Raven shot him in Rocc's momma house after Rocc's funeral. She in jail for it. Holla at me Be-Be," Chucky said, smiling devilishly. Then he turned and walked away.

Luxury Boy Mista was laid to rest on a gloomy rainy day. Many of his friends went to Mista's granny and mom's house and watched Mrs. Gibson, Mista's wife, Ebony, his two daughters, Mrs. Fuller, Kimy, Pelle's wife, and Rocc's wife get in the stretch Navigator to head to the funeral. Pelle, Uncle P, Kev-Loc, and Brown Rag followed behind them in a Platinum Rolls Royce. The funeral felt like deja vu to everyone who recently went to Rocc's funeral. Mista was laid in a special built Platinum Rose casket. Pictures were everywhere of Mista: his wedding, him holding all his kids, and pictures of him and the L-Boyz. People hollered and screamed, "No! No!", and cried when Mista's favorite song, "Stairway to Heaven", was played. Pelle did not go inside during the funeral. He stood outside in the front and smoked Newports back to back. He just didn't want the last time he saw his brother and partner in crime to be in a casket. He wanted to keep the memories of Mista fresher than fresh air ... as all the Luxury Boyz would say to one another. They were all fresher than fresh air. Mista's after burial was held at the same place where Rocc's was held. Pelle got so drunk that Uncle P had to carry him out to the car after the party for the fallen legend Luxury Boy, Mista, was over.

$$\$$$

Three Years Later.

Pelle sat on the edge of his desk at the dealership while talking on the phone with B-Locc.

"Yeah, Pelle, my nigga Lil Q and Yung Money will be there in a minute. I got to bring ten more months. After that we will all be back together and ready for you know who. Yung Money and Lil Q-Baller have piled on the weight. Them lil dudes, big dudes now."

"Oh yeah? Them still my lil nigga's though."

"Man! Come on with that word Pelle … man."

"Look, B-Locc, you being Muslim and all don't mean I'm gonna stop saying 'nigga'. So don't try to change me homie."

"Yeah, whatever Pelle. I'll hit you tonight on the cell. They just called me for a visit with that Honduras girl, Vaness, that Oscar got coming up to see me. She give some bomb head and it's that time again. I'm gone … Seven."

They both hung up laughing. Uncle P went inside the office with Pelle's son, Lil Pelle, and Mista's son. Uncle P and Pelle took them go cart riding every weekend.

"What's up, son and nephew? What y'all wanna do tonight?"

"Ride the cars."

"Alright … Yeah … Uncle Pete, I just talked to Locc. We gone wait till next year — when the yung-ins come home — to get that busta, Big Chucky, so let Kev-Loc and Brownie know to just lay low for now till then. We don't need shit to be hot when they come home."

Chapter 18

For the last six months Pelle's conversations were recorded by Detective Strums. On one of his usual harassment stops, he managed to put a bug on Pelle's couch that was in his office. Sturms sat in his home office and listened to all the recordings of the last six months. He was trying to figure out what location the drugs would be delivered to every month, and how he could get his boss, the captain, to allow his bug to be usable for an indictment in front of a grand jury. Sturms was so fixed on bringing down the Luxury Boyz that his wife of twenty-two years left him and took their two sons with her. So now all he did was think about getting Pelle and all the Luxury Boyz. Sturms grabbed his gun and Jack Daniels whiskey and parked across the street from the dealership, like he did every Friday. He sat there until Pelle and Uncle P left to take the kids go kart riding. Sturms trailed behind the Porsche truck until Pelle lost him with the Porsche's speed.

"Damn it!" he shouted. "I'm gonna get you Pelle! You son of a bitch!"

$

Finally, the time came for the two young guns to be released from prison. The day before their release they did their last dips, pull ups, curls and bench presses with Maniac and B-Locc.

"Make sure you two dudes chill till I get out. Just do y'all halfway house time and start doing you. You know. Don't get violated for living beyond your means. Lay low."

"We is B-Locc. Chill out."

"Don't go out there thinking you swoll, cause you know dudes out there ain't fighting. They shooting. So keep that for those broads. Alright? Cause I ain't gonna accept losing one of y'all," B-Locc spit.

"Alright B-Locc we hear you," Lil Q said, dropping the one hundred twenty-five pound dumb bell.

"I talked to Pelle early this morning. He said he sent two pairs of shoes for each one of you and two fits to dress out in. He said they gone be out there in a stretched Hummer with seven hoes, three topless and four pantiless, to serve you on command."

"Damn! Now that's luxury living right there!" Maniac spit, as he got up off the weight bench.

"Don't trip. Six months from now you gone go home the same way. Luxury Cuzz," B-Locc said.

The next day B-Locc and Maniac walked Lil Q-Baller and Maniac to the R&D building. "I'll holla at y'all later on tonight."

They gave each other the Luxury Boy hand shake. B-Locc and Maniac turned and walked away. Lil Q and Young Money walked into the R&D building to get dressed for release. Pelle had sent a pair of Mauri gators for Young Money and a pair of Jordan's for Lil Q. He sent a pair of ostrich Romeos and a pair of Colby Bryant's, a polo suit and sweat suit for Money, and a Emani suit and a Laker's sweat suit for Lil Q. They both threw on the sweats, not really feeling the suits for a dress out. Two hours later they were processed out and escorted to the front gate. Pelle, Uncle P, Brownie and Kev-Loc stood outside and smoked cigars.

Lil Q and Young Money knew that they were truly free because there were only two guards that walked them out. Pelle told Candy, one of the hoes in the hummer, to step outside. She stepped out topless, grinning from ear to ear.

"Damn, cuzz! You two dudes got big! Eating all that pig in there," Pelle said, smiling.

"Cum-moan homie, you know we don't eat pig. Only pussy," Lil Q said, looking at Candy, and licking his lips.

"Let's roll. Till it's time to come get my other brother that's behind them walls," Pelle said, after everyone gave daps to the new released Luxury Boyz.

Smashin' down the highway on Interstate 10, they popped bottles of Champagne and smoked cigars. Young Money and Lil Q had twenty-four hours to report to the halfway house and three days to get in contact with their probation officers. Lil Q-Baller poured Moet on Candy's titties and sucked it off, while the other girl that sat next to him sucked on his fingers.

"Give that nigga some head," Pelle spit. "or sit on him, uh sumthing. Y'all gotta show my two young-ins a good time on their home coming ride. They should have busted at least seven nuts by the time we hit the city."

Pelle had a party planned at the new club that he just bought in downtown Los Angeles. Young Money and Lil Q would run and manage it along with the promoter that Uncle Pete hired. When they got to the city, they dropped the strippers off at the strip club Pelle had hired them from, then they smashed it to the penthouse high-rise apartment that sat on top of the parlor.

"Damn Pelle, when y'all open a club? Y'all ain't told us nothing."

"I just got it for you and Money to keep y'all out the streets, out of sight, and out of mind."

They jumped on the elevator and got off right inside of the Penthouse.

"Man, back to luxury living!" Yung Money spit. "I'm back!" He screamed.

Everybody laughed.

"Yeah, y'all back," Pelle said. "Now hit the shower and get fresher than fresh air. I got a surprise for y'all."

All six Luxury Boyz were fresh from head to toe when they stepped off the elevator. The buildings personal Luxury Boy garage held a Phantom Rose, an Aston Martin, a Porsche truck, a Jaguar, a GT Bentley, a Cadillac Escalade, and a Mazeradi.

"Whatever cars y'all get keys to is yours except that Phantom. That's mine," Pelle said, getting the keys from the parking security that sat in the garage office.

Lil Q and Young Money each grabbed a key, Money the Mazaradi and Lil Q the GT Bentley. Kev Loc took the Porsche truck key and Brownie the Aston Martin. Uncle

P and Pelle always rode together. Pulling in front of Club Luxury was like a car show. Everybody that was about the luxury life was there including rappers and singers. Pelle, Uncle P, and the promoter, Johnny Boy, had posted posters and aired commercials about the grand opening and home coming party.

The Luxury Boyz jumped out of their cars, handed the keys to the valet and stepped onto the blue carpet that was laid out for them to walk inside the club, as everybody welcomed home Lil Q-Baller and Young Money. Lil Q hollered over the slamming music. He told Pelle that he did his thang. Pelle, Uncle Pete, and some of their favorite rappers and models sat upstairs in VIP area and watched everybody downstairs on the dance floor. Lil Q and Young Money stayed downstairs to party and mingle. Pelle sat in the corner and sipped his Seven-Up with a cherry. He knew that he had to watch the two young-un's that night. So he sat back and talked to a young dude named High Potency, an up and coming rapper. High Potency wanted Pelle to invest in him with his music.

"Yeah, Potency we gonna talk more on that, but not tonight!"

"Alright Pelle. Thanks!"

"Alright homie."

Kelly went and sat next to Pelle.

"I'm bout to leave Pelle. I just wanted to welcome home Young Money and Lil Q-Baller."

"Alright Kelly baby. Tell Lil Mista I'll see him this weekend."

Pelle waved over for Blacc, one of the security body guards to walk Kelly out and wait for her to pulled off. Blacc was going back inside the club when he heard the Big Shug Knight looking dude, which was Chucky.

"Here's $2,000 for me, my homies, and these five fine woman over here!" pointing at the ladies that was staring at the green in his hand.

Blacc walked up to Blue and said, "Let them in. Send them up to the third floor VIP room."

That floor was directly under the floor where the Luxury Boyz were partying. Blacc then went to let Pelle know that the Greenland's were in the building. Pelle-Pelle waved over Kev-Loc and Brownie to let them know about the Greenland's. He told them to bring Young Money and Lil Q-Baller up to the VIP room so nothing would get out of hand. Big Chucky and the Greenland walked through the crowd to the bar. Their loud green clothes caught Young Money and Lil Q's eye. They both were sitting at a table surrounded by seven ladies that they knew before going to the Feds.

"Let's go holler at these fools who's in our club," Money said.

He touched his glock to make sure he had it off safety as he walked toward the bar where Chucky was. Blacc, Brownie, and Kev-Loc walked up on Young Money and Lil Q-Baller.

"Pelle-Pelle said this a safe zone in the club. Let them cats be." Kev-Loc spit. "But we gone get em!"

"Alright," Money spit back, "But we fist to let our presence be known that the young-uns is back, and it's all Luxury in here."

Brushing off the dirt that didn't exist off his Ralph Lauren V-neck sweater. Young Money walked over to where all the Green's were. He called over Brittney, one of the floor waitresses and ordered seven bottles of Rosea. The lights in the club was sparkling off the words, "Luxury Boyz" on the medallion he wore.

"What's luxury Cuzz?" Young Money spit.

Ray Ray, a Greenland Young Money had went to school with, spit back, "Everything's green our way."

"Well homie, just so y'all know, which I know y'all already do. This the Luxury Club. That's what the sign says. It's also a safe zone for us both. So long as y'all here to party and enjoy the luxury life."

Just when Young Money said that, Brittney came and handed out the bottles to the Greenlands. Pelle, Uncle P, and seven more body guards walked up.

"We can buy our own bottles."

Then the Greenland put $5,000 on Britney's tray that held the glasses and bottles.

"What's up?" Pelle and Big Chucky spit with devilish grins.

"S'up! Partner?"

"What brings y'all here to the Luxury establishment and welcoming home party for the young-uns?" Luxury Boy Pelle spit.

"We come to share and throw around some of this green we getting."

"Ball till you fall," Pelle spit. "Let's smash upstairs Luxuries."

He turned. Yung Money, Kev-Loc, Lil Q-Baller, Brownie and Uncle P followed him with the body guards in back of them all.

"Yeah, like yo boy Mista, huh. Heard he got killed by one of his own kind, a bitch."

Young Money reached for his gun but Pelle told him to cool down. Blacc who was a long-time friend of Mista's since school days said, "Yeah, and all that green is for bitches!"

Big Chucky tried to crack Blacc over the head with the Rosea bottle but missed. Instead he caught a right and a left hook from Blacc. Mean Mugg, Big Fella, and all the other security guards rumbled with the Greenlands and threw them out of the club. None of the Greenlands had a gun inside. Blue made sure of that. Being cautious.

Pelle chilled out sipping some Moet for three hours till they rolled. The young-uns took three broads each back to the penthouse apartment, which was the whole tenth floor. That was more than enough room for two football teams. Black, Blue, Mean Mug, and Big Fella watched the Luxury Boyz pull off and was walking around back to their cars when Ray-Ray and Lizard walked up with simi machine guns shooting. They killed Black and hit Big Fella multiple times. Then they escaped in a get-away car that was waiting for them. JB, the club promoter, left Pelle a message about what happened.

Pelle had put his phone down in the master bedroom and was getting a massage from Yvette, the masseuse. She worked at the Luxury Boyz massage parlor that was really a whore house. That was another one of Oscar's money laundering business. Lil Q-Baller walked inside the massive living room that looked like three big living rooms in one. Yvette was sitting behind Pelle massaging his back and neck.

"Damn that's luxury my boy! I need one of those!"
"Yvette will hook you up!"

"Call Cream," Yvette said, she down there. Get your phone. Here this the number. 555-1223. She know who you is. She seen you tonight surrounded by all those girls."

"What y'all was doing in there Q-Baller? Sit ups with weights?" Pelle asked, looking at Q's chiseled stomach, "You got a little size on you Cuzz. We gonna workout tomorrow in the gym when y'all come from the halfway house. Uncle P gonna drop y'all off in the morning."

"Alright, let me go get that massage."

Cream had just got there.

Pelle woke up to the good smell of breakfast. The maid and cook, Sylvania, cooked enough for everyone. Pelle jumped up, showered and then put on some Jordans shorts and a tank top. Then he picked up his phone and checked his voicemail. The first three messages was from his wife and the next five was from Johnny Boy — explaining what happened the night before at the club — then the next one was from Uncle Pete telling Pelle not to trip, because he was gonna handle the problem. He told Pelle to lay low so that he didn't have a run-in with Detective Strums.

"Damn! That nigga Chucky wanna play huh!" Pelle said to himself.

$

Detective Strums sat in front of his Captain and explained how he had slipped a recording chip in Pelle's office and that he had recordings of Pelle talking about distributing drugs and the locations where they pick up their shipments of drugs.

"I know I can bring down their organization. I just need your approval to open an investigation on the Luxury Boyz."

Captain Sparks sat back and looked Detective Strums in the eyes.

"Alright you have three months to bring some solid evidence on the Luxury Boyz. That way we can use the recordings as if you just bugged the office. This can get me into the Mayor's office. Don't fuck this up! You're excused."

$$\$$$

Strums sat in his office and listened to the recordings for the tenth time. He was trying to figure out the times and locations that the loads of drugs came. The times was coded with sports games and the locations changed every time. He picked up his phone and called homicide Detective Flakes.

"Hello!"

"Hey Flakes. Did you get any more information on the Brian Mills, aka Blacc, case?"

"Yeah, I did. You were right, the club belongs to the Corporation Luxury Boyz. Blacc was a body guard for Shapelle Walters, a Luxury Boy. Witnesses say that several body guards got into a confrontation with someone inside the club hours before the shooting. But no one knows anything further."

"Well, I bet Pelle and the Luxury Boyz know who did it but plans on handling it themselves. I'm investigating the organization of the Luxury Boyz crime lords for drug trafficking and conspiracy to murder. So I'll keep you posted and you keep me posted!"

"Ok, Strums. I'll be in touch."

The next six months Strums followed Pelle from business to business and from house to house, even to his home in Alabama where his wife and kids stayed. He was getting more and more information to get an extension on the investigation.

Pelle sat in his office looking over the bills and mail when he noticed a electric and gas bill from Alabama. Putting his thoughts together, he called Uncle Pete and Kev-Loc to take a trip with him to check out the address. When they pulled in front of the house, there was a Impala SS and a SS truck that looked like they needed a wash from not being driven for a long time in the driveway. Kev-Loc jumped out of the car and walked to the front door and knocked. Not getting an answer he walked to the backyard gate but it was chain locked. Pelle called a lock smith to open the house and cars then gave him $1,500 for making keys to the front and back doors of the house.

"I know this was Mista's getaway house. Look at the Cowboy couches. That's been his team since he was a kid," Pelle said.

Everything was dusty. The two bedrooms that Mista or anybody ever slept in looked brand new. Kev-Loc found the keys to both cars in the kitchen hanging up. Then he opened the back door to let the mildew smell out that came from opening the fridge and found everything in it rotten. He looked in the backyard and he saw a shed. He called out to Pelle and Uncle P. Uncle P walked out back to the shed before Pelle. After Pelle finished looking inside the garage, he went to the backyard. In the shed Mista had dry wall from putting money in the walls, fertilizer from burying guns, and a lot of dog food for all the dogs he got trained, and kept at the dealerships and other businesses.

Pelle grabbed one of the slug hammers then went inside the house. He knew Mista would put money inside the bathroom wall first. He found four blocks of wrapped money. In the kitchen he found three more. Uncle P and Kev-Loc dug up the backyard and found two duffle bags full of guns. Pelle loaded his Range Rover with the money. While Uncle P and Kev-Loc put one duffle bag of guns in the trunk of each of the cars that Mista had sitting in the driveway. Kev-Loc grabbed the water hose to rinse the cars but the water was turned off, so he went and grabbed some water out of the fridge and poured it on a towel. He wiped both cars' back and front windows. Pelle-Pelle followed Kev-Loc and Uncle Pete to his house in the next town.

Pelle didn't know that Detective Strums followed them. Detective Strums couldn't see what was in the duffle bags and he didn't have any jurisdiction in Alabama. Strums sat and watched four houses away from Pelle's house. The houses on that block were so big that he sat at the end of the block. Strums called Captain Sparks and explained what he just saw and told him that he videotaped the Luxury Boyz making some kind of pick up. Strums wanted jurisdiction to call the locals to assist in his investigation. Captain Sparks wanted to bring in the Feds but Strums disagreed. He wanted the credit for busting the Luxury Boyz. Captain Sparks told Strums that operation Luxury is now over and to come in with everything he had on them so arrest warrants could be issued.

Pelle counted $3 million in the money counter. Then shipped it in the cars that would be coming in from Mista and Misses dealership. The following morning, they caught a flight to Los Angeles and smashed it to the dealership. Kev-Loc, being the lieutenant of the block, went to Luxury Street and Uncle P made his usual routes to all the businesses. Pelle sat in his plush luxury soft leather seat, lit a cigar and looked up at his best friend's picture that hung over the couch and talked to it as if Mista would respond.

"Damn, Mista you was a cold hustler. I found that out. I'm gonna make sure Ebony get her part and I'mma put a part for Magazine in a trust fund. Oscar will get his mill too. Somedays I wonder if this luxury life is worth the stress, lives, and pain? Now that you seen it all from the beginning and the end, tell me Bro."

Jumping on the cell that couldn't be tapped, Pelle called Oscar.

"What's Luxury Oscar?"

"Pelle good to hear from you. Is everything ok?"

"Yeah, Big O. Thangs just been moving fast. This quarter one mill and five is in route, so you can send the new quarter to the drop!"

"Ok, talk to you later Pelle."

The tap that Strums put under Pelle's desk recorded and was heard at headquarters where narcotics sheriff, Detective Strums, and the FBI sat listening. Pelle jumped on the cell again and told Kev-Loc to have the boys at the drop on Thursday and gave the day of the drop to the FBI and Strums. That night Pelle-Pelle felt like he needed to be around his wife and son. He took a flight to the house and he stayed for two days. He felt something but shook it off.

The next day he called Ebony, Mista's wife, to pick up $700,000 for her and $300,000 for Mrs. Gibson to put in a trust fund for Magazine. Pelle and Kimy went out to eat, shop, and then to the house and chilled like they used to. While lying on Pelle's chest, Kimy told Pelle that she needed him to be around more because she was pregnant again.

"Pelle when you gone give this life up? You don't think you got enough money yet? Or you just gone let the greed destroy you? I need you. These kids need you!"

"I want out Kimy, but I'm in too deep now. This luxury living is for life. I don't know if I'll ever be able to get out. The people that I deal with are very powerful. They may think they need to get rid of me if I want out. You know it's just not as easy as you think."

Wiping the tears from Kimy's eyes, Pelle made love to his wife. Thursday morning Pelle kissed Kimy and his son before getting out the truck. Then he got on his flight to Los Angeles.

Pelle smashed to the dealership to wait for Kev-Loc's call to let him know that everything's Luxury ... meaning the pick-up is done. Detective Strums sat across the street from the dealership in a Range Rover. The agents and deputies were sitting in two Suburban Tahoes. They were all waiting for the "go" from the ATF agents who were tailing and watching the other Luxury Boyz get ready to receive the drop at the liquor warehouse.

"Go ATF!" Agent Sanders said. "Everybody go!"

All of the teams raided their targets at the same time; two houses on Luxury Street, the dealership, the massage parlor, and the liquor warehouse.

"What the fuck," Pelle said, lying on the floor faced down with guns pointed at him. "I'm gonna sue the department for this one."

"I got you this time Pelle-Pelle. I told you I would. This lil bug here will give you life in prison alone, without the drugs from the drop we just seized."

Pelle looked at the bug that Strums pulled from under the corner of his desk and thought *Damn,* but said nothing else.

Everybody that was rounded up from operation Luxury went in front of a Federal Majesty Judge the very same day. Uncle Pete, Kev-Loc, Brownie, Pelle-Pelle, and eight more Young Luxury Boyz and seventeen women from the parlor. After being assigned a judge and given their indictments, they were escorted to a Federal Detention Center to be housed. Pelle called Kimy.

"You have a prepaid call. If you wish to accept this call press five. If you do not wish to receive any more calls from this prisoner press seven. To accept press five." Kimy's heart started to beat faster and faster as she pressed five.

"Hello! Baby!"

"What happened?"

"They raided the dealership this evening babe. They indicted me and twenty something other people on murder, conspiracy, drug trafficking and money laundering. Look Kimy. Call my lawyer and let him know to get down here tomorrow. I got to go. I love you Kimy!"

ABOUT THE AUTHOR

Michael Robinson Jr., aka Mike Mashin, is a up and coming author who wrote his first song at age 7. At that time, he thought he was a singer. Then came along the raps. At the age of nineteen, Mashin and his cousin-in-law, Manky Deuce, started Halfhead Records and the 'Mashin to the Fullest' clique in 1999. He got 2 record deals. one with Spike TV and the other with Reds Records, a company under Spike TV. Mashin was sentenced to federal prison for ten years where he started writing books and also started his publishing company.

Made in the USA
Las Vegas, NV
21 March 2022

46081356R00093